R U 4 REAL?

WRITTEN BY
Nancy Been Peacock

CREATED BY
Terry K. Brown

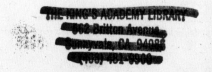

Tommy
NELSON™
Thomas Nelson, Inc.
Nashville

Web Words

2 to/too

4 for

ACK! disgusted

AIMP always in my prayers

A/S/L age/sex/location

B4 before

BBL be back later

BBS be back soon

BD big deal

BF boyfriend

BRB be right back

BTW by the way

CU see you

Cuz because

CYAL8R see you later

Dunno don't know

Enuf enough

FYI for your information

FWIW for what it's worth

G2G or **GTG** I've got to go

GF girlfriend

GR8 great

H&K hug and kiss

IC I see

IN2 into

IRL in real life

JLY Jesus loves you

JK just kidding

JMO just my opinion

K okay

Kewl cool

KOTC kiss on the cheek

LOL laugh out loud

LTNC long time no see

LY love you

L8R later

NBD no big deal

NU new/knew

NW no way

OIC oh, I see

QT cutie

RO rock on

ROFL rolling on floor laughing

RU are you

SOL sooner or later

Splain explain

SWAK sealed with a kiss

SYS see you soon

Thanx (or) **thx** thanks

TNT till next time

TTFN ta ta for now

TTYL talk to you later

U you

U NO you know

UD you'd (you would)

UR your/you're/you are

WB welcome back

WBS write back soon

WTG way to go

Y why

(Note: Remember that capitalization may vary.)

v

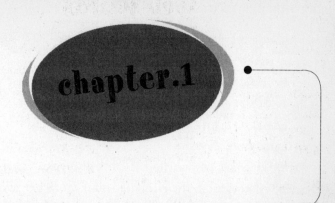

chapter.1

"Uh-huh," Maya said aloud. "I would definitely look fine in that dress."

She moved the computer mouse to the *Print* button and double-clicked the newest fall fashions page on the fashionalley.com Web site. The printer began to whir out a full-color copy of the ivory silk dress.

Downstairs, there was a clatter of drawers being yanked open and closed. Morgan, her fourteen-year-old sister, was searching for her pool pass again.

"Hurry up!" Morgan shouted from downstairs. "Didn't you tell everybody we'd BE at the pool at ten o'clock? We've only got five minutes to get there!"

Maya stretched, turned off the printer, and yelled, "Just as soon as I do my makeup!"

An agonized groan floated up the staircase. "Summer will be over by the time that happens!"

That child is hopeless, Maya thought. *She actually thinks I'm going to set foot outside this house, make an appearance at the pool even, without a perfect face—whatever!!* It was just too horrible to give it any more thought.

Instead, Maya set herself to the task of preparing her face for the day. After rinsing the raspberry mask from her cheeks and forehead, Maya inspected her pores thoroughly in the bathroom mirror. She inhaled deeply and then exhaled, feeling the tingling, healthy glow of her complexion.

"Three weeks until school starts, and you've never looked better," she told her reflection in the mirror. A summer of avoiding greasy French fries and living on crunchy green plants had really paid off. She was lean and mean, and her pores were squeaky clean!

From her treasure trove of cosmetics, Maya smoothed on a mild sunscreen moisturizer with vitamins, adding a pink cream blush over the apples of her cheeks. She lined her lips with neutral pencil and then filled them in with a generous coat of burgundy gloss.

The eyes were her favorite. She lined her lids with black pencil, then traced the bottom lid with the same pencil, and smudged it with a tiny foam-sponge brush. To coordinate with her dark violet tankini, she blended a lavender shadow over her eyelids and finished with two coats of waterproof mascara.

"Maya!" Morgan yelled behind her. Maya's hand jerked, and

the mascara brush fell into the sink. She twirled around and glared at her sister.

"I could have stuck that mascara in my eyeball!" Maya shouted. "How would you like a one-eyed sister to drive you to the pool?"

Morgan threw her sister's beach towel on the floor. "I don't care how many eyes you have. You already act like a cyclops. I'm outta here!"

Morgan stomped downstairs and Maya heard the back door slam.

"Touchy today, aren't we?" Maya said, turning back to the mirror for a final inspection.

Maya eased her lavender silk sarong across the hot black upholstery, turned over the ignition, and backed Mr. Beep out of the driveway. Even before she was born, the ice blue 1972 Volkswagen Beetle had been a member of her family.

Although Maya and Morgan had been born in New York City, their family moved to Edgewood where Mom grew up.

Mr. Beep had been Mom's car when she was a teenager. Now he belonged to Maya. In the last few years, Mr. Beep had grown a fringe of rust around his bumpers. He also needed a new transmission.

Plus, the six months it took Maya to learn to drive a stick shift hadn't done Mr. Beep's gear box any favors. But now Maya was an expert driver, and the money she saved from working at the Gnosh Pit was going directly into the new car fund. No need to tell Mr. Beep, though. It would just make him temperamental and hard to shift.

When they arrived at the Edgewood City Pool, the surrounding grass was a sea of beach towels and sunbathers. Maya spotted Amber, Bren, and Alex in their favorite spot near the pine trees. Alex was the only one who looked up as Maya and Morgan approached the group.

"Did the fashion queen sleep in today?" Alex shouted to Morgan. Morgan rolled her eyes in agreement at Alex.

Maya ignored the jab. She spread her towel in one shake and untied her sarong, letting it fall to the ground. "Okay, what did I miss by being unavoidably detained?"

Bren Mickler lay on her back, her face completely covered with a straw hat.

"The only thing you missed is me being thoroughly depressed," she whimpered from under the hat. "Only three more weeks and then it's back to homework, homework, and more homework."

Bren's familiar back-to-school whining was now officially in full swing. For a cheerleader with a million friends, Bren could complain like a social outcast. At the close of every summer, she elevated moaning to a professional level.

"Okay, listen up," Maya said, pulling a sheaf of paper out of her woven tote-bag. "I've got THE answer to your back-to-school woes. We're going to transform ourselves into rare and beautiful creatures."

Amber, Maya's best friend, laughed and took a few of the print-outs Maya was passing around from her morning's Net search.

"Not bad," Amber said, studying the charcoal kick-pleat jumper and the powder blue pointelle cotton T-shirt.

Maya leaned over Amber's shoulder. "Girl, that is so you!"

Bren Mickler shrieked and held up a color print. "You expect me to wear this?" The print showed a pair of turquoise velvet bell-bottoms that swirled around the model's legs in large balloons of fabric. "This is so hippie-dippy leftover!"

Maya shot Bren a disgusted look.

"Guess again," Maya said, crossing her arms defiantly. "I'll have you know that those pants are the hottest thing out of Milan. You know—Italy?"

Bren grinned. "Well, they are the coldest things in all of Edgewood, Indiana. I'll take a pass on those antiques."

When Maya offered some print-outs to Alex, the scruffy little freshman waved them away. "Oh yeah," Alex said. "Like wearing some goofy outfit is going to make me love school?" Alex paused and then looked at Morgan for emphasis. "Doubt it."

Maya stuffed her pictures back into the straw tote. Alex was as clueless as Morgan. *No wonder those two are best friends,* Maya thought. *Neither one of them care how they look!*

"Morgan!" someone called out. It was Jared, Morgan's friend since the second grade. Maya noticed he was starting to lose the extra weight he had put on in middle school. He and Morgan shared a passion for junk food . . . and long phone calls. They could spend their whole evening on the telephone, entertaining each other with silly jokes and stories about the school day.

Morgan and Alex got up from their towels and threaded their way through the lounging people to join Jared by the pool.

"Explain this again," Bren said, her face back under her hat. "About how buying new clothes will make school less awful?"

Maya shook her head. "Not buying new clothes—modeling them. We're going to put a fashion show together. You know, to show the rest of the fashion zombies at Edgewood High School how to dress with some style."

Bren lifted the hat from her face and peered at Maya. "And just who would come to this fashion show? Only the girls would come, wouldn't they? Guys don't go to fashion shows."

"They would if we had some guys who would model their new fashions," Maya said. "It would be way more exciting to see both girls' and guys' styles."

Bren dropped her hat back over her face. "I don't know. Everybody is getting ready to go back to school, trying to squeeze in everything they put off all summer. I don't think that many people would take the time to go to a fashion show."

"They might if it we put it on in the middle of the back-to-school mixer," Amber said, jumping into the discussion. "The juniors are in charge of organizing that dance. And so far, we don't have any special entertainment to draw people."

As president of the junior class, Amber was always one step

ahead when it came to her official duties. And the best part about Amber—other than being Maya's best friend—was that Amber knew a good idea when she heard one.

"We can call it something cool like 'The Fall Fashion Slam,'" Maya said, her voice dreamy with possibilities. "Everyone will be there."

Bren laughed. "Okay, just as long as I don't have to wear those hippie-dippy pants. Now who are we going to get to model the guys' clothes?"

Maya's eyes scanned the pool and came to rest near the lifeguard chair.

"Check out Brandon and Greg," she replied. "Those two would make great models."

Bren and Amber watched the two handsome seniors as they sauntered to the snack bar. Both guys worked out in the high school weight room, and it showed.

"It's too bad they know how great they look," Amber said. "If only their personalities were as nice as their looks."

But Maya was undeterred. "Who cares about their personalities? All they have to do is show off the clothes. They won't get a chance to say anything. We can have an announcer who will do all the talking. Come on, Bren, you know those guys. Let's go ask them if they'll do it."

Bren stood up and yanked her swimsuit back into place. "Okay. Maya. Just get ready for some serious egomania. These guys are totally in love with themselves."

Maya followed Bren to the snack bar where Brandon and Greg were busily devouring frozen Snickers bars.

"Hi Greg! Hi Brandon!" Bren called breezily. "Did you guys eat up all the Snickers yet?"

Greg laughed. "I think there's one left for you, Bren. Are you sure you should eat one?"

Bren didn't seem bothered at all by his teasing. "Thanks for looking out for me. But no worries. Junk is my favorite food group!"

"Yeah, we know!" Brandon added and ducked as Bren swatted at his head.

"And to think we were going to ask you to model in the back-to-school fashion show," Bren said in a mock-wounded voice.

"Cool!" Greg said. "When is it?"

Maya stepped forward. "We're planning on doing it during the first school mixer. We can get back to you with all the details."

"Definitely," Brandon said. "We're there. Right, Greg?"

Greg smiled at Maya, and she realized she was starting to feel self-conscious. What was that about? Boys never made her feel unsure of herself. Nothing did.

"We were headed into the water to cool off," Maya heard Bren saying. "See you later."

Great, Maya thought. Now she HAD to get wet and completely wreck her make-up. Maya just smiled at Greg, turned and followed Bren to the pool.

Bren dipped her foot into the sparking water and sighed happily. "Ahhhh, feels great. I'm roasting."

"Me, too," said Maya. "That Greg is a serious hottie."

Bren turned and studied Maya. "Look who's got a crush!"

Maya smiled and brushed the comment away with a flick of her wrist. "Don't be silly."

Bren dove into the pool and surfaced next to where Maya stood. "Come on, Maya! Get WET!"

Maya heard Brandon and Greg behind her, walking toward the pool. Now she really had no choice but to jump in. She leaped into the pool as delicately as a gazelle, feeling the cool water envelop her body as she sank in a profusion of bubbles and then glided effortlessly to the surface.

As her head rose out of the water, she heard Greg's voice: "What a cannon ball! There goes half the pool water!"

Maya felt something grab in her chest. Was Greg saying that about her? She hadn't had one candy bar the entire summer!

Maya tried to act nonchalant, pushing off the side and gliding across the width of the pool in a few side strokes. But inside, she was still wounded from Greg's remark.

How dare he say that? She wasn't fat! Was she?

chapter.2

"Earth to Maya! Earth to Maya!"

Maya realized that Bren was trying to get her attention. They were back lounging on their towels, catching the remaining rays of the late-afternoon sunshine. Amber had packed up and left a half-hour ago to meet her mother at Edgetowne Mall for some back-to-school shopping. Morgan and Alex were off somewhere, probably hanging out with Jared.

"What is with you?" Bren continued. "You've been on the moon ever since we talked to Brandon and Greg. You HAVE got a crush on Greg, haven't you?"

"That muscle-head?" Maya snapped. "No way!"

Maya studied her legs, stretched out in front of her. Her body was small and strong, her legs shapely and firm. Okay, so maybe her legs did get slightly wider at the top of her thighs, but so what? Did that make her a cannonball?

Maya yanked at the bottom of her tankini. Had this thing somehow gotten smaller? She never washed it in the washing machine. She'd always followed the instructions that came with it: Rinse in cool water and hang to dry.

"Hey, can I get a ride home in the Beep-mobile?" Bren asked, breaking into Maya's thoughts again. "Amber gave me a ride this morning."

"Sure," Maya answered absent-mindedly, looking around to see where Morgan had gone.

They gathered their towels and totes and signaled to Morgan that they were ready to leave. Maya needed to be home early today—again. Every time her mom went to a faculty party, Maya got stuck with the thankless job of fixing dinner.

More often than not, her mom went to those faculty events by herself, since Mr. Cross was usually tied up managing his restaurant. But Maya's friend Jamie Chandler had offered to work from noon through the Gnosh Pit's dinner hour so that both of Maya's parents could attend the get-together. It seemed weird, as if Jamie were playing Cupid or something with Maya's parents. Maya wondered if Jamie made the extra effort for Mr. and Mrs. Cross because Jamie's own dad had left his family when she was only eight years old.

Back home, Maya made her way into the kitchen, turned on the gas burner, and began browning chicken breasts in a skillet. She heard the back door open and then a loud thud—Jacob, her older brother, had tossed his football gear on the floor. He lumbered through the kitchen without stopping, moving like someone who had just crossed Death Valley on foot.

"When's dinner?' Jacob mumbled.

"Not even an hour," Maya replied.

"Whatever it is, make a lot of it," Jacob said and disappeared into the family room. Maya heard the TV come on and the distinct sound of the remote methodically clicking past commercials until it stopped on CNN Sports.

Maya opened a can of diced tomatoes, then quickly chopped an onion. She poured them over the chicken, sprinkling the whole mixture with soy sauce. Although the recipe called for canned mushrooms, Maya decided to use the fresh ones in the refrigerator. *Not as much sodium,* she reasoned.

Morgan ambled into the kitchen and froze. "Mushrooms!" she gasped, pointing at the neat sliced pile on the chopping board. "Maya, you know I hate mushrooms!"

"If you don't want to eat mushrooms, then pick them out," Maya said, stirring the simmering skillet.

"No way!" Morgan protested. "They taste like dirt! I'm not going to eat that garbage!"

Maya was ready to throw her wooden spoon at Morgan. Instead she pulled herself together and turned back to the stove.

"Fine," Maya sniffed. "You can starve for all I care."

At that moment, Dad and Mom strolled into the kitchen,

arm in arm and smiling over some shared joke. But their smiles faded as soon as they heard the girls arguing.

"Mom! Maya's cooking *mushrooms!*" Morgan wailed.

Dad and Mom gave each other knowing looks and sighed.

"Party's over," Dad said dryly, retreating into the family room.

Mom crossed her arms and gave Maya and Morgan "the look." It was an expression they had seen many times before. Loosely translated, "the look" meant, "Would either of you like to explain how this got out of control or shall we just pretend it never happened?"

After a prolonged pause, Mrs. Cross broke the silence. "Thank you for making dinner, Maya," she said quietly. "Morgan, I would appreciate it if you'd set the table."

Both girls knew their argument was finished.

"Mom," Maya said. "I need to ask you something. Privately."

Both Maya and Mrs. Cross looked at Morgan.

"Okay. I'm leaving," Morgan said and wandered into the family room.

Mrs. Cross returned her gaze to Maya. "I'm listening," she said, gently folding her arms across her chest.

Maya searched for the right words. "Do you think I look, uh, maybe a little heavier now than I did a couple months ago?"

She could see that her mother was puzzled by the question.

"I don't think you look the least bit heavy," Mrs. Cross replied. "Why would you think such a thing?"

Maya told her about the incident at the pool with Greg.

Mrs. Cross nodded thoughtfully. "You know, honey, most African-American women like the way their bodies look. We are proud, and it shows in the way we carry ourselves. I'm surprised at you. Your body is beautiful, Maya."

"Just like your mama," Mr. Cross said as he walked back into the kitchen, wrapping his arms around his wife. "All of the women in this house are beautiful."

Maya smiled. "Oh, Dad. You would say that no matter what."

Mr. Cross tried to look insulted. "Are you telling me I don't know beauty when I see it?" he said, putting on an attitude.

"You're a beautiful girl," Mrs. Cross added seriously. "No two ways about it."

Maya realized how silly the whole weight issue sounded when she said it aloud. "Okay," she smiled. "I just needed to get that out of my head."

The next morning Maya was up, showered, dressed, and painted by 8:30 A.M.—Amber had scheduled a 9 A.M. meeting with Mr. Carson about the back-to-school dance. Maya wanted to get his permission for the fashion show as soon as possible.

At 9:05, Amber and Maya were sitting in Mr. Carson's office. The principal looked more relaxed in his summer attire—pale green golf shirt and khaki slacks.

"You called the meeting, Miss Thomas," said Mr. Carson. "What's on the agenda for today?"

Amber handed him a sheet of paper. "These are the main

points we need to cover for your approval," she said. "There's the candy sale and the junior homecoming float. But first we wanted to talk about the back-to-school mixer. Maya has a great idea."

Amber looked at Maya and nodded.

"Okay," Maya said, springing into action. "We want to spice up the dance with a fashion show. All the latest fashions for girls and guys. We'll use students to model the clothes so that everybody sees how nice they could look if they made an effort."

Mr. Carson nodded. "I like it. Our students might enjoy dressing a little spiffier this year. Will this be expensive? And, how will you get these clothes for the students to model?"

Maya smiled. "I've got that all worked out. We can get the clothes from local stores, and then give them free advertising by telling the students where they can buy everything."

To be perfectly honest, Maya hadn't actually contacted any stores yet. But she didn't want to mention that to Mr. Carson. Besides, she wasn't at all concerned about the stores going along with it. Who would want to turn down free advertising?

"Well, it sounds like you've done your homework on this project," Mr. Carson said, using his favorite expression. "I guess I don't want to stand in the way of progress—"

There was a loud knock on the principal's door, and Bren stuck her head inside.

"Hi, Mr. Carson!" she said. "Is it time for our meeting? Hi you guys! What are you doing here?"

Mr. Carson looked at the clock on his office wall. "Bren,

your appointment isn't until 9:30. But come on in. We might as well get this all hammered out at one time."

Amber and Maya gave each other a puzzled look. Meg DeLoss and Bren, two of the school's eight varsity cheerleaders, walked in wearing their new fall uniforms.

"The cheerleaders wanted to use the back-to-school mixer to build school spirit for the football season," Mr. Carson explained. "They suggested leading some of their new cheers at the dance."

"Wouldn't it be cool?" Meg bubbled. "We could do all the cheers we learned at camp this summer!" She launched into a syncopated clapping rhythm and started chanting: "Oh yeah! Oh yeah! Go team! Go team! Uh-huh! Uh-huh!"

Maya managed a polite smile. "That seems like a lot of entertainment. Maybe even too much for one dance."

Meg stopped abruptly and her expression soured. "Oh, really? Well who wants to see a bunch of weirdo outfits? Not me!"

Bren and Amber started to speak, but Mr. Carson held up his hands. "Ladies, ladies! Either we can work this out in a peaceful way, or we can cancel this entire event. But first and foremost is this: we set a cooperative example for the rest of the student body. Do we all agree on this?"

The four girls nodded, but no one spoke. Maya didn't want to say anything that might jeopardize the fashion show. But adding a pep rally in the middle was just about the worst idea she could imagine.

"Good," Mr. Carson continued in his most diplomatic voice. "May I suggest that we combine forces and have the cheerleaders model some of these clothes? And we save the cheers for our first pep rally against Bloomington?"

Although he had put his suggestion in the form of a question, Maya knew better than to argue against including the cheerleaders. Besides, she would need more models for the show anyway. Maya decided to take the lead in salvaging the show.

"That sounds great," she said. "We will need to get a few more guys for models, too. Brandon Gallagher and Greg Muir have already agreed to be in the show."

Meg brightened again. "Greg Muir? He is SO cute. I think he has a crush on me."

"I think he has a crush on himself," Maya said, still irritated by his behavior at the pool.

Mr. Carson stood up and rubbed his hands together, signaling the end the meeting. "Thanks ladies. I think this will work out just fine. Keep me posted."

The girls stood up in an awkward silence and walked into the hall. Bren finally broke the ice. "Just let us know what you need for the fashion show," she said.

"Sure," Maya replied, forcing a smile. "I'll be asking for everyone's sizes so we can start getting clothes."

Meg seemed cheery again. "Maya, if there are any his-and-her fashions in the show, can I wear them with Greg? We would look so totally cute together!"

Maya thought about the his-and-her T-shirts they sold at the fair. Both shirts were printed with an arrow pointing sideways and the announcement, "I'm with Stupid."

"I'll have to get back to you on that," Maya said, stifling a smile. "We haven't made any decisions yet."

The cheerleading captain called from down the hall to Meg and Bren. Meg bounded down the hall, leaving Bren, Amber, and Maya together.

"What can I say?" Bren apologized. "She's got a major crush on Greg."

"Gee, do you think so?" Maya said, clasping her hands and batting her eyes longingly. The three of them laughed.

"Are we meeting on the Web site tonight?" Amber asked.

"Wouldn't miss it," Maya answered. "We've got a ton of work to do if this show is going to be a success."

For the rest of the morning, Maya sat in her room, telephoning stores at Edgetowne Mall and explaining her idea for the fashion show. But none of the managers seemed willing to lend the clothes.

"I would have to get approval through our division headquarters," one manager said. "And that could take several weeks."

Another store manager was adamant: "When these clothes come back missing buttons or with make-up on them, how am I supposed to sell them to a customer at full price?"

An upscale boutique manager told Maya, "The only items I could loan you would be my summer fashions on the clearance rack. Would that help you?"

"Thanks, but I don't think that will work," Maya said, trying to hide the disappointment in her voice.

"Let me know if you change your mind," the boutique manager said in a sympathetic voice.

"Okay, sure," Maya said absently. "And thanks again."

Maya clicked off the portable telephone and sat on her bed brooding. Now where was she supposed to get all those outfits? Especially since she had already told Mr. Carson that getting the clothes was a done deal. She felt foolish for having told Mr. Carson her plan before it was final. And she felt angry with those managers, too. Students were buying back-to-school fashions hand over fist, spending their hard-earned lifeguarding, burger-flipping, and table-serving wages at all of those stores. But none of those managers were grateful enough to loan her anything.

Maya started her computer and went to the fashionalley.com home page. All those cool clothes now seemed out of reach. Glumly, Maya clicked through the pages of skirts, boots, outrageous sweaters, jewelry, and hats.

The phone rang and Maya mechanically picked it up.

"Hullo."

"Hi honey, it's Mom. I know it's Morgan's turn to start dinner, but I just remembered she has a doctor's appointment in a half hour. Run and tell her to get ready, and I'll pull in the driveway in about ten minutes. If she's ready, we can still make her appointment on time."

"Okay."

There was a pause on her mother's end. "What's with you? You sound down in the dumps."

Maya couldn't bring herself to tell her mom how the show was disintegrating piece by piece. This whole event was falling apart. Thanks to the meeting with Mr. Carson, the show was being invaded by cheerleaders. But that shouldn't matter now because she had no clothes to model anyway. "I'm okay," she told her mom. "Just a little tired. Bye."

She clicked off the cordless phone and shut down her computer.

"Morgan," she called.

No answer.

"MOR-GAN!"

No answer.

Now I gotta track her down, Maya fumed silently. On her way out of the room, Maya almost stumbled over the bathroom scale, sitting in the middle of the floor. Rather than step over it, she stepped onto it and looked down. The red needle came to a stop and Maya squinted down at the reading: 122 pounds.

Impossible! She jumped off the scale as if it were an electric hotplate. One hundred twenty-two pounds! After spending the entire summer at 115? No way! Maya bolted down the stairs, shouting for Morgan. She found Morgan out in the backyard in a chaise lounge, painting her toenails with silver glitter nail polish.

"What did you do to our bathroom scales?" Maya shouted.

Morgan looked up from her painting handiwork. "What did I do with the scales?"

"The scales are all wrong!" Maya hissed. "What did you do?"

Morgan looked at her sister as though Maya had just turned a shade of neon green. "Oh, yeah. Blame me 'cause you've got a big butt."

Maya flew at Morgan like a hawk catching a field mouse. "Come here, and I'll show you," Maya said, grabbing Morgan's wrist and yanking her off the lounge and across the yard.

"My toes aren't dry!" Morgan yelled, walking on her heels through the grass, the nail polish brush still gripped in her fingers.

"Come up here and weigh yourself," Maya ordered, hauling Morgan up the stairs to their room. When they got to the scales, Morgan stepped onto them, looked at the dial, and stepped off.

"They're fine, "Morgan said.

"They can't be!" Maya wailed.

Morgan got back onto the scales. "Yeah. They're fine. A hundred and thirty pounds. That's what I weigh."

This was some kind of bad dream. There had to be an explanation. "There is NO WAY I am 122 pounds," Maya sputtered. "Absolutely no way!"

A car horn sounded in the driveway. Morgan looked at Maya.

"Who's that?" Morgan asked.

A sick feeling rose in Maya's stomach. She looked at Morgan in bare feet, cut-off jean shorts, and a faded T-shirt with the paint spots still fresh from her art class mural project. Not exactly the fashion statement Mom would expect for the doctor's office.

"I am losing it," Maya moaned while the honking grew longer and more insistent.

chapter.3

Maya thought her head would explode from the honking.

"That's MOM!" Maya shrieked. "I was supposed to tell you she is picking you up for a doctor's appointment. You are going to be SO late . . ."

Morgan was already pulling off her paint shirt and kicking off her jean shorts in one wriggling motion. In the next moment, she was hopping one-legged out of her bedroom, hiking up a clean pair of khaki shorts, trashing her toenails, and pulling a clean T-shirt over her head. Maya raced down the stairs ahead of her and was apologizing at the driver's side window of her mom's car as Morgan leaped into the passenger seat.

The car flew into a reverse turn, and after a micro-second

stop at the end of the driveway, roared off toward the doctor's office. Maya's mom was boiling.

Watching the car speed away, Maya heaved a weary sigh. *Better fix dinner before I forget that, too,* she decided.

When they returned from the doctor's office, Mom didn't lecture Maya. Instead, she went upstairs, changed out of her work clothes, came back downstairs, and put her arm around Maya's waist.

"How's my baby doll?" Mom asked, giving her a squeeze.

"I'm sorry, Mom," Maya began.

"I know you are," Mrs. Cross said. "Thanks for fixing dinner two nights in a row. You're the best."

Once the family was seated for dinner and had said grace, the food was passed around the table. Mr. Cross offered Maya the butter for her potato.

"No thanks, Dad," Maya said.

Mr. Cross stopped and studied his daughter. "You're gonna eat that potato dry?"

"Sure," Maya said brightly. "Tastes great—less fattening."

From the corner of her eye, Maya saw him raise his eyebrows. Mom knit hers into a V. It was as if her parents could speak whole sentences to each other without uttering a word.

Maya heaped her plate with salad and crunched the greens.

"Excuse me, Miss Bunny Rabbit," Mr. Cross said, extending the bottle of salad dressing he had just used. "Would you care for some dressing on that salad?"

"No thanks, Dad," Maya said. "I don't need the fat."

Mr. Cross began to speak, but Jacob interrupted.

"You better pour some of that dressing on your lamb chop," Jacob said, chewing laboriously on the meat. "This stuff is so dry, it tastes like old shoe leather!"

All four Crosses turned and looked expectantly at Maya.

"I left all the fat ingredients out," Maya said cheerily. "No need to clog up our arteries with oil and grease."

Mrs. Cross put down her napkin and stared at Maya. "This has something to do with the scales being in the middle of the hall floor, huh?"

Maya felt herself starting to crumble from within.

"I'm getting fat," Maya said, bitterness seeping into her voice. "I'm turning into a blimp and nobody cares." Maya pushed her chair back, stood up, and glared at her family. "You're trying to make me fat by feeding me butter and salad dressing. Can't you all see how awful I look?"

Her dad looked as though he had been punched in the stomach. "I can't believe what I'm hearing," he murmured.

Maya ran out of the kitchen, bounded up the stairs, and fell on her bed. How could she possibly run a fashion show when she was turning into a human beach ball? It was as plain as the numbers on the bathroom scales. All her careful dieting over the summer had been a complete waste. She buried her face in her pillow and forced herself not to cry.

About twenty minutes later, Maya heard the dishwasher

starting its cycle, water running in the sink, and footsteps coming up the stairs.

"We need to talk," Mom said from the doorway. Maya rolled over as she felt her mother sit down on her bed.

"Morgan told me all about the scales," Mom continued. "And I'm wondering where you got the notion that 122 pounds is out of line for an active girl like you?"

"It's right there on the chart," Maya said, pointing to her desk.

Mom picked up the computer print-out and studied it. "These weight ranges seem a little skimpy to me," she said. "Where did this weight chart come from?"

"The NYCModels.com Web site," Maya recited.

Mom studied the chart for awhile in silence. "You are comparing your weight against adults whose job it is to be paper thin? I wonder how many of those stick-figure models could compete in the butterfly or freestyle swimming events with you. They would snap in half before they finished the first lap."

It was true that Maya had improved her times in both events over the summer. Breaking that 00.55-second school record in freestyle had been one of the best memories of the past year.

"I wonder if this fashion show is such a good idea," Mom said. Maya couldn't think of a good response, so she said nothing.

"I'll make you a deal," Mom said gently. "If you can get this whole weight thing in perspective, then the fashion show can go on. But if your weight becomes more important than the fun of modeling clothes, there will be no show. At least no show for Maya Cross. Understood?"

Maya nodded. She didn't want her mom to know that there was no fashion show because there were no clothes. At this moment, the whole event was turning into an unqualified disaster.

"Welcome to TodaysGirls.com!" her screen said in purple and silver letters. Maya clicked a little box at the bottom of the magenta screen and typed in Maya003, her password to the Web site.

Amber's Thought for the Day immediately popped up:

When five sparrows are sold, they cost only two pennies. But God does not forget any of them. Yes, God even knows how many hairs you have on your head. Don't be afraid. You are worth much more than many sparrows. Luke 12:6–7

Bottom line, no freaking. Whatever it is you need, God will remember to give it to you!

After her rotten day, Maya felt like a sparrow all right—one that had been blown out of the air by a shotgun. But she clicked into the chat room, determined not to tell the others how bad things really were. Instead, she would be upbeat and motivating. And somehow, she would save this train wreck of a fashion show.

Maya typed into the dialog box.

nycbutterfly: hey fashion babes!

The cyber chat flashed across the screen.

rembrandt: kewl—ur finally here! chic sez u had a good meeting w/ Mr. C today

faithful1: yeah, except that ALL the cheerleaders will be in the show. Sorry chic!!!!!!

chicChick: NBD, faith . . . Meg just gets on my nerves L

nycbutterfly: BTW, can we talk about the show???? it is less than 3 weeks away!

rembrandt: FWIW, i don't think i can help out much. i'm working doubles at the Gnosh till school starts . . . need the $$$ for art camp next yr.

nycbutterfly: that's kewl, rembrandt. just as long as you can be in the show

faithful1: do you need any help picking up the outfits from the stores?

nycbutterfly: no—i think the 1st thing we need to talk about is body weight. i found a chart on the net that every 1 needs 2 C.

chicChick: ????? isn't that what the clothes r 4? 2 cover up our bodies???

nycbutterfly: u r 2 funny NOT!!! every 1 should come over 2morrow and weigh in. or would u rather be embarassed 3 weeks from now?????

chicChick: WHATEVER!
jellybean enters the room
jellybean: hi! whazzup?????
chicChick: fashion newz!!! we have to report for weigh-
    ins at ur house 2morrow.
jellybean: thazzOK . . . no 1 weighs more than i do!!!
faithful1: OK after we weigh in, what then?
nycbutterfly: the rest is ez . . . i'll take care of the clothes
    part.
faithful1: i'm happy 2 help u.
nycbutterfly: no thanx. got it under control . . .

Some control I've got, Maya thought. *How am I gonna find all
those clothes in three weeks?*

rembrandt: CUL8r i promised jessica i'd play w/her
    before her bedtime. BFN
rembrandt has left the room

Maya didn't care much for kids, but Jamie's nine-year-old sister Jessica was cool. Even if she always roped Jamie into playing
board games with her in the evening before bed. Jamie's mom
was back in school, trying to finish her law degree at night. So
Jamie helped her mom as much as she could.

nycbutterfly: kewl rembrandt! CU 2morrow for weigh in

. . . around 10 a.m.?

TX2step enters the room

TX2step: whats this weigh in stuff?

jellybean: we r all getting weighed 2morrow 4 the fashion show.

TX2step: NW

jellybean: it will B fun TX! we can pick out some kewl clothes.

No way! Maya thought as she read her sister's chat line. *Those two fashion flunk-outs are NOT picking out their own clothes. Better kill that notion right now . . .*

nycbutterfly: all clothes worn in the show must be approved by the style committee.

TX2step: and who, pray tell, is on the committee?

nycbutterfly: well i'm the head of the committee.

TX2step: yeah . . . the head AND the tail!!!!!!!!!!

nycbutterfly: just be here 2morrow around 10 a.m. TTYL

Maya signed off. Alex could be so irritating! Maya couldn't see how Morgan could put up with her for a best friend. *If there's one thing I cannot stand,* Maya brooded, *it is a bossy know-it-all like Alex.*

It was still dark outside, and someone was shaking Maya's shoulder. "Wake up," the person whispered. "Come on, wake up!"

Maya opened her eyes enough to see Bren standing next to her bed.

"Uh?" she mumbled. "What time is it?"

"It's early, okay?" Bren said, her voice agitated. "What difference does it make? Just get up and weigh me so I can be long gone when everyone else comes."

Maya collapsed back into her pillow. "Go away. Come back at ten."

"I will not," Bren growled. "If you expect me to get weighed, then you've got to keep this whole thing a secret. I've been pigging out all summer, and I don't want the whole world to know what I weigh."

Maya was just about to tell Bren how ridiculous that was, until she remembered that she hadn't told anyone except Morgan about her seven-pound weight gain. And other than telling Mom, Morgan swore to Maya that she hadn't blabbed about the seven pounds to anyone else.

"Oh, alright," Maya said, pulling herself into a sitting position on her bed.

"Step on that scale by my desk."

Bren stepped onto the scale, read the dial, and sighed with relief. "Whew—128 pounds. I was worried. But that's only three pounds over what I usually weigh. Not too bad."

Maya was reading her Internet chart. "Not too bad unless you see that at five-feet, seven inches, you should be in the 115 to 120 pound range."

Bren looked shocked. "What?" she said, grabbing the chart. "No way!"

Maya sat silently and watched Bren find her height and weight category on the chart.

"Don't freak out," Maya said. "With some exercise and a good diet, you can shed those ten pounds with no problem."

"Ten pounds?" Bren gasped. "I'm only three pounds overweight."

"Not according to *this* chart," Maya said. "And don't give me that look. I didn't make up these numbers."

Glumly, Bren handed the chart back to Maya. "Don't tell anybody! Okay?"

Maya held her hand up. "Sworn to secrecy. Now can I go back to sleep?"

Bren nodded. "See ya."

Maya pulled the covers over her head. "Good night."

The next weigh-in participant was Jamie, arriving shortly after Maya woke up.

"Sorry," she said as she bounded through the back door. "I've got a million things to do today, and I thought I would take care of this now."

"Sure," said Maya, sipping a glass of orange juice as she led Jamie up the stairs to the scales.

Jamie's weight came in precisely at 120 pounds. When Maya announced that she was six pounds over the acceptable range, Jamie's jaw dropped.

"Don't worry," Maya said. "We are all about to embark on a serious regimen of healthful food and exercise. We can lose this weight in plenty of time for the show."

"I guess so," Jamie said. "If I can squeeze all of that into the next three weeks."

Amber was the only one who arrived at Maya's house precisely at 10 A.M. "Where is everybody?" she asked, looking around the kitchen.

"Apparently you are the only one who remembered when the actual weigh-in was supposed to be," Maya said. "Everyone else got here earlier. Of course, Alex hasn't shown up yet. Not that I expected her to be here on time."

Amber was a pound lighter than her normal 120, but Maya quickly pointed out that 119 was still nine pounds too heavy for Amber's height range on the chart.

"There is *no way* I can lose nine pounds that fast," Amber said with an easy smile. "But I'm more than willing to drop a pound or two."

"If you really follow the plan I have for all of us, it should be easy to lose nine pounds," Maya said.

Amber looked skeptical. "I don't know, Maya. Coach Harrison—"

"Coach Harrison!" Maya exclaimed. "That's who we need

for this. He knows all about buoyancy and body fat. He can give us some good suggestions."

"Okay, Maya," Amber said. "I just don't want to get carried away with all of this weight garbage. The clothes are what people will want to see. Not us."

"You let me worry about the clothes," Maya said.

After the swim team's pre-season meeting that afternoon, Maya signaled everyone to follow her into Coach Short's office.

"Aren't you all sick of hearing me talk today?" Coach joked as the girls squeezed into his small office.

"We wanted to ask about body fat," Maya said. "We're trying to lose weight for the back-to-school fashion show. We wanted to know how to calculate body fat in our total weight."

"Oh, no!" Alex groaned and rolled her eyes to the ceiling. Alex hadn't shown up for the weigh-in at all. Maya was thoroughly disgusted with her.

"Maya, you girls better be careful," Coach said. "Your body can't even function without a certain amount of body fat. Women must have between eight and twelve percent essential body fat in order to have normal body function. And up to twenty-five percent body fat is considered okay for a grown woman."

"Fine," Maya said. "If you can show us how to calculate our body fat ratios, we can see where we fall on the charts."

Coach looked around the room. "Are you all as interested in finding this out as Maya is?"

All the girls except Alex nodded.

"Okay," Coach said. "But I don't want some crazy fashion show to get in the way of our team exercise and eating the right foods. Is that clear?"

"Perfectly," Maya said. "And to make it interesting, we are going to divide into teams. Amber, Jamie, and Bren can be on one team. Morgan, Alex, and I can be on the other. The team in the best shape by the fashion show gets first pick of what to wear."

"I don't want to be on her team," Alex said aloud to Morgan. Morgan gave Alex the "we can talk about this later" look.

At Coach's direction, the girls used skin-fold calipers to take measurements on their upper arms, waists, and thighs. Then each girl wrote the numbers on a sheet of paper and gave it to Maya.

"Okay," Maya said. "I'll have these percentages figured up by tonight. Are we chatting tonight?"

"Can't," said Jamie. "Gotta work late."

"Count me out," Bren said. "The cheerleader sleepover is tonight at Meg's."

"Probably," Amber said, "but after family time."

"I have to give my dog a bath," Alex said.

"You don't have a dog," Morgan said, taking a playful swing at Alex.

As it turned out, no one was in the chat room that night. *And after all the work I did figuring up everyone's body fat percentages,*

Maya grumbled. She was about to sign off when she remembered that her "What's Hot . . . What's Not" area of the Web site had not been updated for nearly a week.

Clicking onto her fashion page, Maya deleted the makeup tips, and then thumbed through the new issue of *FashNews* magazine, looking for a tidbit to use.

Other than a small item about lip liners, Maya couldn't find anything worth writing about. *Unless I list the body fat numbers,* she thought, pulling the folded papers from her shoulder bag.

"Amber . . . . . . 122 lbs . . . . 20.7 body fat," Maya typed into the page. "Jamie . . . . 125 lbs . . . . . 21.9 body fat . . . Morgan . . ."

chapter.4

All the girls were in the chat room the next morning. However, the conversation was anything but chatty.

chicChick: HOW COULD YOU??????????????????
nycbutterfly: sorry . . . . i didn't think it was any BD . . .
. . . . hey i posted my weight on the weight chart 2!
faithful1: yes but U chose to do that. we didn't have any choice
rembrandt: that's why i freaked when i saw the numbers. i felt like a piece of meat on that chart!

With everybody on Maya's case, she decided it was time for damage control.

nycbutterfly: i guess i thot that it didn't matter because we all know so much about each other. C what i mean?

faithful1: yes but do U C Y we r mad at u for doing it?

Amber was right. Last night it seemed like a perfectly good idea. This morning it seemed, well, like a not-so-good idea. There was only one way for Maya to dig herself out of this hole.

nycbutterfly: FWIW, i'm sorry. will u 4give me?

faithful1: FWIW, yes.

chicChick: yeah, i still luv ya!

jellybean: we can still have fun with this fashion show, if we all work 2gether.

TX2step: NW i'm getting weighed. C what happens when U do?

nycbutterfly: hey i just said i was sorry!

TX2step: that and 59¢ gets you a taco.

jellybean: will u 2 stop it??????? can't we B nice 2 each other?

rembrandt: jellybean is right. we need 2 get along!

TX2step: i will if she will.

That little twerp! Maya growled to herself.

nycbutterfly: CU at the pool this afternoon?
faithful1: i'll B there at 3.
chicChick: me 2
rembrandt: gotta work at 4. maybe 2morrow . . .
jellybean: TX, r u coming over for lunch?
TX2step: in 1 hour. CYA

Alex and Morgan didn't know it yet, Maya decided, but their personal exercise program was about to begin.

Around noon, Maya heard the two girls downstairs, eating sandwiches in the kitchen. She casually walked in, opened the refrigerator, and poured herself a glass of cranberry juice.

"As soon as you two are finished, we can start on our workout," Maya announced.

Alex squinted at her. "What workout?"

Maya smiled sweetly. "If we're going to win this contest, we've got to start working out together."

Alex and Morgan seemed not to hear Maya's voice.

"The contest," Maya repeated. "You know—to see who gets in the best shape for the fashion show."

Alex studied the ceiling and said nothing.

"Okay," Morgan said. "In a minute."

Maya went upstairs and sat down at the computer. She selected a graphics template and titled it "fashion show 3."

Next, she created a invitation she could e-mail to all the fashion show participants:

You are invited to the
Kick-off Rehearsal for the

Back-To-School Fashion Slam

Noon in the EHS gym on Monday, Aug. 24th

"Are you guys ready yet?" Maya yelled downstairs.

"In a minute," Morgan answered.

When we get back from the workout, I'll e-mail the invitations. But before I do that, I'd better move the body weight and fat chart from the Web site. I definitely don't need any more flak.

After moving the documents into her own files, Maya turned off the computer and went downstairs. Morgan and Alex were lounging on the kitchen chairs, munching cheese doodles.

"Enough junk food!" Maya announced. "We're jogging to the park and back."

"Come on Maya, we just ate," Morgan whined. "Let's start tomorrow."

These two had to be the laziest slugs on earth. "We either jog today, or you walk to the pool this afternoon," Maya said. "So you're gonna be exercising one way or another."

"You can't make her walk," Alex said, not moving. "Your mom would make you drive her to the pool because she can't drive yet."

What a little know-it-all that Alex was. "Well, I might have to drive Morgan to the pool," Maya replied. "But I sure don't have to drive you anywhere. So if both of you want a ride to the pool, you had better get up and start moving."

Alex didn't budge.

"Come on," Morgan said wearily. "Might as well get this over with."

Alex and Morgan rose from their chairs like ancient Egyptian chattel, off again to build some pyramids. Maya jogged triumphantly out the back door and down the driveway, with the reluctant girls in tow.

The sun overhead beat down through the cloudless August sky. Only the shade trees provided a momentary respite as the three jogged toward Edgewood City Park.

By the time they reached the pavilion at the park entrance, all three were soaked with sweat. They waited in line at the drinking fountain, too thirsty and exhausted to speak. After they had each slurped down some of the tepid fountain water, Maya tried to lighten things up a little.

"I think I just shed a pound of sweat," she announced. "Kinda feels good, doesn't it?"

"Oh yeah," Alex replied. "I haven't felt this good since I cracked my ribs in a bike wreck."

Maya smiled graciously, ignoring the comparison. "Let's head back, get our suits, and drive to the pool."

Morgan held up one hand. "You guys go on ahead of me. I can't jog all the way back to our house. I've got a cramp in my side."

Maya decided to be generous with her sister. "I'll jog on ahead and wait for you guys at the house."

She set off down the sidewalk, maintaining an easy pace until she reached home. Their big old house was surrounded by tall oaks that provided instant heat relief as she hit the yard. Like a canopy above, the trees shielded the sun, as well as afforded a cool breeze on most summer days. Maya went upstairs, took a quick shower, toweled off, and put on her tank-ini and sarong.

After pulling her hair back and clasping it in a metallic alli-gator clip, Maya applied a sunscreen moisturizer, some berry cream blush, plum lip gloss, and just a hint of champagne eye shadow. Then she feathered some mascara on her top and bot-tom lashes.

Looking out the window and down the street, she saw no sign yet of Morgan or Alex. This was taking longer than she had imagined. So Maya sat down and e-mailed all of the rehearsal invitations to everyone on the list. She was just finishing when she heard the girls walking into the kitchen.

"I'll be right down," Maya called. She turned off the com-puter and grabbed her beach tote. That pool was going to feel wonderful today.

Amber and Bren were sunning themselves on the grass when Maya, Morgan, and Alex pulled into the pool parking lot. Morgan and Alex dropped their towels and went to find Morgan's friend Jared.

"I took my team for a jog after lunch," Maya announced.

Bren laughed. "The only jogging we've done is to the snack bar and back."

Amber smiled at Maya. "When is our first rehearsal?"

"Monday at noon," Maya said. "I e-mailed invitations to all of our group, the cheerleaders, and Greg and Brandon. This is going to be the coolest way to start the school year."

Bren rolled over, sat up, and surveyed the crowd of sunbathers. "Do you realize that in two weeks, we'll be sitting in study hall, remembering the joy of hanging out at the pool on a beautiful day like this?"

Maya studied Bren. "You can be downright depressing. You should find a way to get pumped about school starting. Don't you think so, Amber?"

Amber started to say something, then stopped as Morgan and Alex returned to where the girls were sunning on the grass. "Jared had to leave early today," Morgan said, clearly disappointed.

"Too bad," Maya said absently. "That reminds me. We're going to have to find a few more guys to model in the show."

"What about Jared?" Morgan said, brightening. "He's so cool. He does this funny walk that cracks me up."

"Are you kidding?" Maya snorted. "He's way too fat to be in our show. We want buff *guys*, not buffaloes!"

Instead of laughing, Amber and Bren looked at the ground and didn't say anything.

"That's mean!" Morgan shouted. "Jared is a cool guy. I don't care if he is a little heavy. At least he isn't a creep like Brandon and Greg."

Maya looked at Amber for support, but she just shook her head and said nothing.

"You know, all I'm trying to do is find some model-quality guys for this show," Maya said.

"That doesn't give you the right to trash her friend," Alex shot back.

"Okay maybe I shouldn't have called him a buffalo," Maya said. "But that still doesn't mean he can be in the show."

No one said anything. After a few moments of uncomfortable silence, Morgan headed toward the pool with Alex trailing behind her. Maya sighed, picked up a fashion magazine, and thumbed aimlessly through it. A sense of discomfort hung over her the rest of the afternoon.

That evening, Maya got in bed early and browsed through a stack of magazines. There just had to be a way to get some clothes for the show. And soon.

Maya had drifted off to sleep when she felt someone shaking

her shoulder again. She opened one eye and saw Morgan's worried face.

"Wake up Maya," Morgan said. "This is bad."

Just the way she said those six words set off an alarm in Maya's chest.

"What are you talking about?"

"You know those invitations you e-mailed?" Morgan asked.

"What about them?"

"The invitation e-mails were all sent with documents attached to them," Morgan said. "The attached documents were the weight charts."

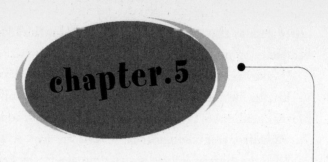

chapter.5

In just fifteen seconds, Maya went from calm sleep to wide-awake terror.

This can't be happening. I'm having a nightmare. Maya thought. "How? How could that be?"

Morgan looked as miserable as Maya felt. "I don't know. But about a half hour ago, I checked my e-mail. And there was a message from you with an attachment that was labeled 'Fashion Show.' And when I clicked on it, there was the weight and fat chart."

Maya clamped her hand over her mouth. How could this have happened? How could she have attached those weight charts to the invitations? How could she have been so stupid?

Maya scrambled out of bed and clicked on the power button of her computer. Her fingernails tapped nervously on the corner

of her desk as she waited for the screen to go through its pre-
dictable booting up routine.

As soon as the e-mail program was activated, Maya clicked
on the *Sent* file and scrolled to the most recently-sent list. There
they were, all neatly lined up for inspection: e-mail address after
e-mail address with the Fashion Show attachment. Maya's hand
shook as she clicked on the e-mail attachment for Greg Muir:
bicepman@muscleguy.com

Like an ugly joke unfolding before her, the screen blos-
somed with the familiar colorized chart listing the body weight
and fat of each of Maya's best and closest friends. And there
were Maya's big, fat statistics, too, for Greg, Brandon, and all
the cheerleaders to read and laugh at and enjoy over and over
again all weekend before the first rehearsal at noon on
Monday.

All Maya could do was stare at the screen, one hand pressed
over her lips, and feel her heart pounding like that of a fright-
ened animal, trapped inside her chest.

"What are you gonna do?" Morgan whispered.

Maya shook her head. "I don't know. I've never messed up
this bad before."

Morgan put her hand on Maya's shoulder. "I'm sorry, Maya.
I wish I could help."

Maya put her hand over Morgan's. "Thanks, Morgan."

Neither spoke as Maya closed the screen and hit the *Get
New Mail* button on the e-mail menu. Her screen flashed,

"You have 12 new messages" and began listing them down the window: faithful1, rembrandt, chicChick, megacheer, bicep man . . .

"I can't read these right now," Maya said softly. "I think I know what they say anyway."

"Good idea," Morgan said, her voice laden with pity.

Maya closed the e-mail program and sat staring at the empty screen. The only sound was a chorus of crickets, chirping outside somewhere in the night.

Finally Morgan spoke. "Do you want me to stay up with you for awhile?"

Maya tried to smile. "That's okay. You can go on to bed."

Morgan patted her sister's shoulder again. "Well, g'night."

Maya nodded. "Yeah. G'night."

Maya passed most of the weekend in a daze, refusing phone calls and getting on the computer just long enough to see if anyone else had sent new mail. She feigned illness for most of Saturday, describing vague pains that traveled from one vital body organ to another. Mostly, she stayed hidden in her room.

By Sunday evening, Maya had constructed an elaborate plan to move to New York City and work as a waitress. She would stay with her godmother until all of the people in her class had graduated and moved away. Then she could return to Edgewood in disguise and live out her days as a shriveled up, poverty-stricken short order cook at the Gnosh Pit, hiding out in the kitchen.

"It's what I deserve," she told Morgan, "for being such a moron."

"I don't think Dad or Mom would go for that plan," Morgan said. "They still think you're going to college."

"I'm too big of an idiot to go to college," Maya said morosely.

From the downstairs hall, Dad called up the stairwell: "Maya! Morgan! Time for dinner."

Maya shook her head. "Tell them I'm still sick."

Morgan nodded and left the room. About ten minutes later, Dad appeared in Maya's doorway.

"Daughter number two tells me that daughter number one is unable to make an appearance at the dinner table," he said. "And this is because daughter number one sent some unfortunate e-mails. Have I got it right so far?"

"It's not funny, Dad," Maya pouted. "My life is over."

"Well, now," Dad said, sitting down in Maya's desk chair. "That was a pretty short life you had. Did you forget about going to college and getting a degree in broadcast journalism? How are you supposed to host the Today Show if the only thing on your resumé is a part-time restaurant job?"

Maya almost smiled at that. When she was a little girl, she would "interview" her parents, pretending to be Jane Pauley at first, and then later, Katie Couric. But that was before her life came to an untimely end on Friday night.

"How can I face all of them tomorrow?" Maya asked.

Her dad grinned. "You may find this hard to believe, but I've made a complete fool of myself more than once in my life. And after it happens, the only thing you can do is to say to yourself, 'I will *never* do that again!' Then you gather up all your courage, you go back in there, and you do what you gotta do. People respect it when you admit your mistakes. And somehow, you make it better."

Maya thought about it. Her dad could make any idea sound possible. Even the ridiculous notion of showing up at the gym tomorrow for the rehearsal.

Dad gave Maya a hug. "In the meantime, come on down and sample some of my shrimp jambalaya. Mighty fine, yawl! I gare-on-tee!"

Probably just to make Maya feel better, her parents stretched out the Cajun accent thing all through dinner, but by the time Morgan brought out the apple-cinnamon beignets, all five Crosses sounded like they'd just floated up to Indiana from the bayou.

After dinner, Maya typed a short letter of apology to Bren, Amber, and Jamie. To the cheerleaders and the boys, she typed another letter, explaining that the chart had been sent by mistake. Then she deleted every e-mail in her in-basket without reading them.

As she was turning off the computer, her dad stuck his head into her room.

"I need to drive up to Fairview to pick up some paper products for the Gnosh," he said. "I could use some company. Wanna ride along?"

Maya listened to her dad sing Motown hits on WGOR, the golden oldies radio station, all the way to Fairview and back. His smooth tenor eased her mind, and she couldn't help wondering how those old songwriters knew *just* what to say . . . lyrics about leaving troubles behind and having faith in tomorrow.

When they arrived home, it was almost 10 o'clock.

"Thanks, Dad," Maya said.

"You're welcome, Jane Pauley," Mr. Cross answered with a smile.

"That's *Katie Couric,* Dad," Maya smiled back.

Maya sat in Mr. Beep on the far edge of the school parking lot, waiting for everybody to arrive. When her watch read 12:10 P.M., Maya opened the door and took out the portable stereo with the music she had been taping over the summer.

She walked purposefully across the parking lot, through the main entrance of the school, and down the hall to the gym. She took a deep breath, let it out, and opened the gym door.

Brandon and Greg were shooting baskets at the far end of the gym. The cheerleaders, including Bren, were splayed out on the floor in a circle; stretching and extending their already flexible bodies into even more flexible shapes.

Amber, Jamie, Morgan, and Alex were lounging on the bleachers nearby. Maya walked directly over to the group and put down the stereo.

"Thanks for coming today," Maya said nervously. "Let's just

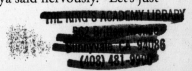

try and get through this rehearsal. I know you guys must hate me."

Morgan was the only one who spoke. "Nobody hates you. We all know it was an accident."

"Thanks, Morgan," Maya said, looking at her hands. "Well, I guess it is time to get started."

Maya picked up the stereo and took it to the front of the gym. "I need everyone's attention, please! Will everyone come to the front so we can get started?"

As the students moved to form a semi-circle around Maya, she saw Brandon whisper something to Greg, and both of them grinned. The cheerleaders were all wearing the same amused expression on their faces.

"All right, people," Maya said, speaking to everyone and making eye contact with no one. "We need to practice moving to the music so we won't feel self-conscious on the night of the fashion show. So I'm going to put on the music I've been taping for the show. Then, when I call your name, you need to walk along that red stripe on the floor until you reach the foul stripe down there. Then come back up here and get in line to do it again."

Greg stuck his hand in the air. "Excuse me, Ms. Director, sir. Will this help us lose weight? My thighs are just enormous!"

Brandon and Greg exploded into gales of laughter. The cheerleaders turned various shades of purple, trying to hide their laughter. Jamie, Amber, and Alex stood with their arms crossed in a stony silence.

"Okay, I'm going to start the music," Maya said, pressing the play button and cranking up the volume to cover the boys' laughter. "First model: Meg DeLoss."

Meg sprang to life, strutting to the disco-era music as she moved down the red stripe.

"Next," Maya shouted over the music. "Greg Muir."

Greg leaped onto the red line, gyrating to the music like John Travolta in *Saturday Night Fever*. Brandon doubled over, howling with laughter.

"Next," Maya shouted. "Morgan Cross."

Morgan stepped out shyly from the group. She found the red line and then walked carefully along the line as if she were teetering on a balance beam.

"Next," Maya shouted. "Alex Diaz."

Alex must have been waiting for this moment. The minute she found the red line, she began dancing a sailor's hornpipe all the way down the gym, like something right out of a Popeye cartoon. Brandon and the cheerleaders howled their approval.

Maya watched Alex as she danced—everyone else clapping in time as Alex's feet slapped the floor. And Maya wondered how they could enjoy this impromptu display so much when it looked so incredibly silly.

"Next," Maya shouted wearily. "Brandon Gallagher."

Brandon couldn't wait to strut across the floor, flexing his muscles and winking at all the girls who were watching him.

"Next," Maya shouted, wishing she were anywhere but there. "Amber Thomas."

Amber took her place on the red stripe and walked down the line in a completely natural, understated way that somehow managed to stay in time with the music. After she reached the end of the runway area, she turned and looked at Maya.

"Thank you," Maya mouthed gratefully.

Amber smiled shyly and walked to the back of the line.

Bren and Jamie both did their walks with complete ease and calm, keeping effortlessly with the rhythm. Maya held up her clasped hands in appreciation to both of them when they finished.

She ran each of the cheerleaders through their walks and then turned off the music.

"Okay, everybody, let's gather around here for some information," Maya said. "I think we've all got the idea of how to move down the runway in time to the music. We'll have more practices in the next two weeks so that we can all feel comfortable."

Meg stuck her hand in the air. "When are we getting the clothes? We think we should be allowed to pick out our own stuff. We want to look *good*. Right?"

The other cheerleaders buzzed in agreement.

"I still have some loose ends to tie up on the fashions we'll be wearing," Maya said. "We can talk about who'll be wearing what at next Monday's rehearsal."

Meg looked unhappy but didn't say anything.

Brandon stuck his hand in the air.

Maya rolled her eyes. "Is this a serious question?"

"Oh yes," Brandon said, his face angelic. "But won't *some* of us be modeling clothes from the Edgewood Awning and Tent Factory?"

The cheerleaders screamed with laughter as Brandon and Greg waddled around in small circles, their cheeks blown out like balloons.

"Well, if that is the end of the comedy routine, I guess we will see everybody next Monday," Maya said. "Thanks for coming."

Maya unplugged the stereo and joined her friends. "I would apologize right now, but my head is about to split in half. If anyone is still talking to me, I'll see you on the Web site tonight."

She walked out of the gym, down the hall, and into the sunlight. From where she stood, the world had not changed at all. The sky, the houses, the trees—everything was the same. Good old dependable Edgewood. She closed her eyes and exhaled slowly, releasing three days' worth of tension. And she realized she was going to be alright.

"Thanks, Dad," Maya said aloud.

chapter.6

U gh," Maya shuddered. "Not that ugly thing."

Maya was standing in front of her open closet, surveying the collection of clothes that made up last year's school wardrobe. She remembered the day she first saw, fell in love with, and had to have this long jacquard knit skirt with the tiny triangle print of pink, white, and gray.

She must have worn this skirt a million times last year. It reminded her of every sophomore language arts test and biology lab sheet she had ever completed. That skirt was like the Smithsonian exhibit of the First Ladies' inaugural ball gowns: it had come to represent every moment of her sophomore year.

The sweaters, pants, and tops hanging in her closet gave Maya the same rush of nostalgia. Each one had a memory attached to it—drama club auditions, track meets, a speech given at the United Nations Day assembly. It was as if, on the last day of school, her clothes had been sealed off in a time capsule and buried in the closet all summer. Now she felt like a tomb raider, unearthing artifacts that were better left undisturbed.

"Time for some new clothes," she said aloud.

Mom had agreed to take her daughters shopping tomorrow at Edgetowne Mall. From past experiences, Maya had figured out that shopping trips with Mom were always more enjoyable when Maya had prepared a complete list of what she needed before they ever set foot in the store.

It wasn't that Maya's mother was no fun on shopping trips. It was just that being a full-time professor, Dr. Cross wasn't accustomed to wasting large amounts of time. Not like Amber's or Bren's moms. Amber's mom was more than willing to spend most of a day finding just the right skirt and sweater combination. And Bren's mom could easily while away the morning trying on shoes at four different stores.

But when Maya would strike a variety of poses in the dressing room mirror, asking her mom if she really, really, REALLY liked this T-shirt, then Maya's mom would rub her eyes and her mood would sour to a combination of weary and irritable.

"I've already told you that I like it," Mrs. Cross would say. "And I've been cooped up in this dressing room so long, I'm starting to forget what the outside world looks like. Make a decision and let's go."

Morgan was the easiest person on earth to take shopping.

She would sit in the dressing room all afternoon under a mound of clothes, nodding and telling Maya how great she looked in every single thing.

Thanks to Amber and Bren's moms, those girls already had their back-to-school clothes bought and hanging in their closets. *And that,* Maya thought, *might just save me a whole lot of trouble.*

Maya closed her closet door, grabbed her clipboard, and popped her disco tape into her purse—just in case. All the girls were meeting at Bren's house tonight, each with an outfit that might work for the show. Maya hadn't told anyone that her mall connection had fizzled. But maybe if their new school clothes were good enough, she wouldn't have to come up with a whole new wardrobe for the fashion show.

Bren's house was the perfect place to meet. They always had their sleepovers there, too, because Bren had her own suite on the second floor. In addition to a huge bedroom and bath, she had a living area with a big-screen TV, a curving sectional sofa with *two* hide-a-beds, and a kicking stereo system.

When Maya, Morgan, and Alex arrived at the Mickler's, Maya recognized the Thomas' Isuzu Tracker parked in front of the garage. Jamie must have gotten a lift with Amber.

"This house is unreal," Alex said, climbing out of Mr. Beep's back seat. "Bren's room is as big as my whole house."

"Go to medical school like Bren's dad," Maya said. "Then you can buy one of these houses, too."

"No way," Alex huffed. "I'm not even going to college. You couldn't pay me to go to medical school."

"Suit yourself," Maya said. "I don't think water skiers or rodeo queens make this kind of money."

The three of them walked up the landscaped sidewalk to the front entry and rang the bell. The first seven notes of the Indiana University fight song chimed, and Bren's mom answered the door. Cita Mickler was a beautiful woman. She had met her husband while scuba diving in the Philippines. So romantic. Maya admired Mrs. Mickler for her exquisite taste in clothes and her enthusiasm for whatever project the girls were planning.

"Hi girls!" Mrs. Mickler said. "Everyone is upstairs. You know the way."

"Thanks, Mrs. Mickler," Maya said.

When the girls reached the top of the steps, Jamie and Amber were watching the large-screen TV, and Bren was on the portable phone, gabbing away. When she saw Maya, she grinned and waved. "I'm sorry," she told the person on the other end of the phone. "I've gotta go. Can I call you back later?"

"Who brought clothes?" Maya asked loudly.

Jamie looked sheepish and shook her head. "Everything I own is old and boring. And I haven't spent a penny yet on school clothes. I'm trying to save all my cash for art camp next year. Clothes just seem like such a waste of money."

"No problem," Amber said. "We're the same size. I brought some new stuff. Let's go try it on, and see what you like."

"Thanks, Amber," Maya said. "What about you, Bren?"

Bren grinned as she clicked off the telephone. "If it's made by Gap, it's in my closet. My mom and I like went absolutely nuts a few days ago. When we first got to the Gap, there was this really cute clerk there. And he so *doesn't* go to Edgewood. He's a *senior* at Rushville. At least I think he said Rushville. Maybe he said Shelbyville. No, I'm pretty sure he said Rushville."

Maya listened impatiently, waiting for Bren's narrative to return to the subject of clothes.

"Anyway, he was like 'wait till you see this,' and I was like 'well let's see it already,' and he dragged out all their new fall stuff from the back of the store—right off the truck! I think he said his name was Andrew. Yeah, it was Andrew. Okay, so I tried on a bunch of things. Everything looked perfect, and he made Mom laugh the whole time, so we ended up buying a whole ton of clothes."

"Sounds good," Maya said, silently thanking God that Bren had finally taken a breath. "Now go dig through that ton of clothes and pick an outfit for the show."

Morgan and Alex flopped down on the sectional sofa, kicked off their sneakers, and propped their feet on the large ottoman. "We'll be the audience," Morgan said. "We don't have any new clothes to model anyway."

Maya sat down on the sofa, throwing off her sandals, and putting her feet up too.

"Okay," she yelled in the direction of Bren's bedroom, "let's see what you got!"

60

Jamie emerged shyly from the bedroom, wearing a pair of lightweight wool, pinstripe pants and a capsleeve, cotton stretch lavender sweater. "Well," she asked. "What do you think?"

Maya leaned back into the sofa. "What can I say? That is a great look on you."

Jamie smiled. "Really?"

"Sure," Maya said. "Do you have any shoes you can wear with it?"

Jamie's smile faded. "All I've got are my clogs. But they're black so they would look pretty dressy."

Maya frowned. "I can't see clogs with that outfit. Could you buy some chunky heels with a strap back?"

"Come on, Maya," Jamie chided. "I'm not buying new shoes for this show. No one is going to see my shoes anyway. These pants are long enough that it doesn't matter."

"I think it does matter," Maya insisted, making notes on her clipboard. "Let me see if I can find some shoes that work."

Jamie shook her head and disappeared into Bren's bedroom.

"Let's see some more clothes out here!" Maya yelled.

Bren came out, wearing a wheat-colored jean skirt and a pastel-striped knit top with a ballet neckline and raglan sleeves. It was cute enough, but certainly not fashion show material.

"Out of everything you bought from a cute guy, *this* is the most interesting outfit you could find?" Maya asked.

Bren looked confused. "Well, no. I was just thinking

that—for a school fashion show—it might make sense to wear something, you know, down to earth and—"

Maya interrupted her. "I'm not looking for down to earth, Bren. I'm looking for memorable, sensational clothes that will dazzle the audience. So go back into your closet, dig through that zillion-dollar wardrobe of yours, and find something more visually stimulating. Okay?"

Bren shrugged. "Okay. Sorry."

"Don't worry, Bren," Maya said. "You'll get it right the next time." Suddenly Maya felt a pang of guilt about her own irritable tone—until Alex opened *her* mouth.

"Attention everyone," said Alex, in a sports commentator voice. "The fashion dictator has spoken."

Maya angrily ignored Alex. "Amber?" Maya called toward the bedroom. "Did you find something to model?"

Amber walked out of the bedroom in a matching cashmere skirt and sweater. With her honey-colored skin, she looked stunning in deep coral.

"Now *that's* what I'm talking about," Maya said directly to Alex. "That's an outfit."

"There's only one problem," Amber said. "I borrowed it from my cousin. And she's taking it with her to college in three days. But she said she got it at J. Crew in the mall. So you can just borrow this outfit from J. Crew for our show. Right?"

Maya was caught off-guard. "No problem." Maya wasn't

about to admit, especially in front of know-it-all Alex, that none of the stores could loan her any fall clothes.

Amber smiled. "Great. So at least Jamie and I have something to wear for the show. Now we need to find something for you four."

"Morgan and I can wear real clothes, like overalls and cords," Alex said, her voice edged with defiance. "We aren't going to parade around in some dorky skirt."

"If you want to be in *this* fashion show," Maya replied, "you are going to wear something that's actually in style. It isn't going to kill you to wear current fashion."

"You're right," Alex snapped. "It isn't going to kill me because I'm not going to wear whatever the Fashion Dictator tells me to wear."

"Maya and I can figure all that out later, okay?" Morgan interjected, heading off another argument between the two. Alex set her jaw and turned her attention to the big-screen.

Bren came back into the room, wearing the shorts and top she had been wearing earlier. "I don't know what to wear for the show," Bren said. "It really doesn't matter either way to me. Why don't you just get something from the mall, and I'll wear it?"

Maya felt a momentary panic and then let it subside. "No problem," she said, surprised at how convincing she sounded. "That way all the clothes will have a continuity to them. We can include some dressy outfits, some sporty ones, maybe even some party dresses."

Bren smiled. "Cool. Is anyone else thirsty? Let's go downstairs and get some soda."

They filed downstairs into the huge kitchen. But when Bren opened a two-liter bottle of Mountain Dew, Maya wrinkled her nose.

"I don't need the calories," she said, grabbing a bottle of Perrier water.

Everybody peered into their empty drinking glasses with a pang of momentary guilt, and then held them out for Bren to fill with Mountain Dew.

"You're all hopeless," Maya said.

"Whatcha doin'?" Morgan had wandered into Maya's room and sat in the white wicker chair next to her four-poster double bed.

Ever since they had returned from Bren's house, Maya had been surfing the Net, looking for the perfect clothes for each model in the fashion show. She had printed her favorite ensembles for each girl and was now in the process of scouring the guys' fashion pages for Greg and Brandon's clothes.

"What do you think about these outfits?" Maya asked.

Morgan looked at the computer screen from across the room. "Those look good to me."

"You can't even see them from over there," Maya protested. "Come over here and look."

Morgan got up and walked around the bed to where Maya was hunched in front of the computer. Maya was surrounded by pages of print-outs from dozens of different Web sites. On some pages, Maya had written the names of the students in the fashion show.

"Are these the clothes we're getting from the stores at the mall?" Morgan asked.

Maya snorted. "Listen, you are the only person who knows this, but we can't get any clothes from the stores at the mall. They gave me a million reasons why they won't loan us any. But the bottom line is, they won't."

Morgan looked puzzled. "So where are we getting all the clothes?"

"Here!" Maya said, pointing to her computer screen. "This is the only place left. And I have the fashion world at my fingertips."

Morgan looked even more puzzled. "These places won't loan any clothes to us. They don't even know us."

Maya smiled as if she were in on a marvelous secret. "Of course, they'll loan us the clothes. We buy them, we use them, and then we return them. It's the same as if they were loaning them to us. We just return them after the show. They'll never know the difference."

Morgan sat down on the edge of the bed. "This is crazy, Maya. We could get in real trouble for this. You could lose all the money in your savings account. If you even have enough money to do this."

Maya dismissed her with a wave of her hand. "Online

shopping doesn't work with cash. And I don't have a credit card. So I'll just use this."

She held up a credit card with her mother's photo on it.

Morgan gasped. "Mom's card? Have you lost your mind?"

"All I have to do is return those outfits within two weeks and the charges will all be taken off the account," Maya said. "It will look like a mistake from the credit card company. And if I buy the clothes online, I can just type in the credit card number, and no one has to know if I own this card or not."

"Don't do this," Morgan urged in low, fearful tones. "This is like stealing."

"It would be like stealing if I weren't going to return all the clothes," Maya reasoned. "But all I'm doing is borrowing Mom's credit card so I can borrow some clothes for the show. So you see? This is just borrowing."

Morgan stared at the floor and said nothing.

"What am I supposed to do?" Maya said. "How can I tell everyone that we have no clothes? It isn't my fault that those stupid stores at the mall won't loan us anything."

"Ask Mom for help," Morgan said. "She might be able to think of some way to get the clothes from the mall."

Maya shook her head. "You know what Mom will say. She will tell me to use the clothes we're buying for school. But no one wants to see us parading around the gym in some boring old clothes. What kind of a fashion show is that?"

Morgan started to say something and then stopped.

"Don't worry about this," Maya said. "I've got it all figured out. Just don't go telling Mom, or I really will get in trouble. I don't need her on my back, too."

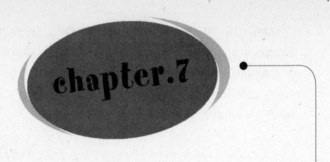

chapter.7

Maya was up early, showering, putting on her make-up, and doing her hair. A trip to the mall was always worth the extra effort that it took to look perfect. Last night, while scouring the Net for online shopping sites, Maya had found some tantalizing products: boots and handbags and body lotions and colorful shawls and hats and—well, the possibilities were nearly endless.

Mom said they would leave the house around 11 A.M. It was only 9:30 when Maya applied the final strokes of polish to her toenails. Then she sat down to let them dry and logged on to the TodaysGirls.com Web site.

As always, Amber's Thought for the Day popped up immediately:

And why do you worry about clothes? Look at the flowers in the field. See how they grow. They don't work or make clothes for themselves . . . So you can be even more sure that God will clothe you. Don't have so little faith! *Matthew 6:28–30*

It's okay for daisies to just hang in the field. They don't think about being roses—they're happy just being themselves. Take it from God, we're already taken care of as his beautiful flowers!

If only I were a beautiful flower, Maya thought. *Then I wouldn't have to worry about losing weight before the night of the show.* Her thighs seemed to stubbornly cling to every ounce, refusing to shrink no matter what she did.

Clicking Amber's window away, Maya hit What's Hot . . . What's Not and posted some of the names of the new sites she had discovered last night. Then she typed in:

Fashion Tip #1: Eat only healthy non-fat foods until the day after the fashion show. Fashion Tip #2: Read Fashion Tip #1 again, and PAY ATTENTION THIS TIME!!!!!

Special note to Morgan and Alex: I have scheduled a workout for 8 p.m. tonight. Be at the Cross house no later than 7:45 p.m.

Maya printed out her wish list of back-to-school clothes and accessories. She knew her mother would never agree to buy everything on the list. But at least she could try to get most of it. And when she didn't get everything on the list, her mom could give her Speech Number 42: it is so much better "to choose a few nice things instead of buying a lot of junk."

Maya went downstairs to wait for her mother to come home. Mom had an early morning seminar that finished at 10 A.M. She would be back soon.

Morgan was sitting at the kitchen breakfast bar, eating a bowl of cereal. Maya poured a glass of orange juice and sat down next to her sister.

"Did you make a list for shopping today?" Maya asked.

Morgan grinned. "Nope. I know what I want. Same as last year, pretty much."

Morgan ate another spoonful of cereal. "Did you order those clothes off the Internet last night?"

"Yes I did," Maya said. "And I would appreciate it very much if you would not bug me about it. What's done is done. Besides, you'll thank me when you see what I ordered for you."

Morgan looked squeamish. "I'm not sure I want to know."

The sound of a car coming up the driveway made both girls gulp their last mouthfuls and hurriedly straighten up the breakfast bar. As soon as Dr. Cross dropped her briefcase in the den and checked her phone messages, the three were off to the mall.

"Where to first?" Mom said, scanning the upper levels where most of the cool shops were.

Maya held up her list for her mom to see. "You can start almost anywhere."

Mom laughed. "That looks like the list you made for Santa Claus one year. It was so long, you used about three feet of your dad's adding machine paper just to write it all down."

Her mom had repeated that story at least a hundred times, but it never failed to make Maya smile at the memory of it. "I couldn't help it," she teased back. "My writing was big. I needed all that room."

"What about you, honey?" Mom said to Morgan. "Where's your list?"

Morgan smiled. "I just want to get some jeans and sneakers. I hate buying winter clothes when it's still hot outside."

"I do, too," Mom said. "And let's save some time for French onion soup and salad at Le Bon Maison Café."

Morgan found jeans right away and a short-sleeved yellow top that happened to be on sale. Maya tried on some olive drab khakis. They fit, but she wasn't sure she liked the color.

"Your list does specify dark khakis," Mom said, reading it in the dressing room. "And they really compliment your figure. I think they're cute."

Maya studied herself in the mirror. "I know I said dark-colored khakis. But I wonder if these are too dark. These dressing room lights are different from real light."

"Why don't you walk out into the store and look in a mirror out there?" Mom said. "If you promise not to wander around the store, I'll wait here. Just go out and look and come back."

Maya went outside the dressing room to look at herself in a three-way mirror. But another girl and her boyfriend were taking up the whole mirror, discussing a new coat the guy was trying on.

"Hi!"

Maya turned around and nearly bumped into Greg Muir.

"Oh, hi!" Maya said, recovering from the surprise and trying to seem pleased. "Doing some shopping?"

"Yeah," Greg said, eyeing the pants that Maya was wearing. "Are you buying those? They look great."

Maya was astonished. Greg—the dude who had made her feel just like a beach ball—was now telling her that she looked good? Maya felt herself blushing.

"Thanks," she said. "I don't know if I like the color or not."

Greg just grinned. "The color? Why don't you like the color? Don't you like green?"

Maya grinned. "I like green. I just thought that maybe they were too military, if you know what I mean."

"They look fine to me," Greg said. "I mean the green looks fine."

Maya couldn't think of anything else to say.

"Thanks," she said finally. "I guess I'll buy them."

"You should," Greg said, smiling.

Back in the dressing room, Maya smiled at her mom.

"I really want these pants," Maya said.

"They must look a lot better out in the store," her mother said.

"Oh, yeah," Maya answered. "A lot better."

At the next store, Morgan tried on sneakers and Maya scoped out boots, thinking about Greg. Maybe he only acted like a jerk when he was around Brandon. Greg certainly seemed different when it was just the two of them talking.

Mom paid for Morgan's sneakers and then the three of them headed for Lannings, the big department store on the main concourse. As they were walking by the bookstore, Mom stopped and peered at one of the displays.

"There is that new book on African art history," she said. "I want to run in and get a copy. I'll be right back."

Maya and Morgan waited outside while their mom disappeared into the bookstore. Both of them knew better than to go inside with her. Their mother could spend hours browsing through the rows and rows of shelves. The only thing that would make her hurry was to stay outside.

"Guess what?" Maya said. "I ran into Greg Muir when I was trying on pants."

Morgan rolled her eyes. "He's such a jerk."

"I don't know," Maya said quietly. "He's not so bad."

"Are you kidding?" Morgan said. "Since when is he not so bad?"

Maya shrugged as her mom came out of the bookstore, smiling to herself.

"Shall we, girls?" she said, picking up a shopping bag and leading the way to the next store.

Lannings was having its annual Back-to-School Super Sale and throngs of customers were crowded into the different departments. The entrance to the store featured cosmetics and fragrance counters.

"I need some new mascara," Maya said. "Can we get it at the Mystique counter?"

"Mascara?" Mom said. "You can buy mascara anywhere. We are buying clothes today. Remember?"

"But I need this Mystique mascara," Maya said. "It's the only protein-enhanced mascara on the market."

Mom gave Maya a look of exasperation. "You know perfectly well that you can't absorb protein through your eyelashes," Mom said. "You really are becoming a sucker for all of those commercials."

"The protein is in the color, Mom," Maya insisted. "This mascara was developed by Swiss scientists to stay on longer."

"If you want protein-enhanced mascara, you can pay for it out of your savings," Mom said. "I refuse to pay a fortune for protein-enhanced mascara. What else is on your list?"

Maya pointed to the designer label section, where dozens of people were going through the racks of clothes. "I wanted to show you some great clothes over there."

"Can we eat first?" Morgan said. "It looks really crowded over there."

Mom looked at Maya. "How about it? Let's take a break and come back."

Maya was about to protest, but her mom and Morgan looked ready to wilt.

"Okay," Maya said. "I could use a salad."

While they were waiting for their food, Mom pulled out the book she had just bought.

"I read about this book in *The New York Times Book Review*," Mom said, slowly turning the pages. "There are some excellent shots of Ashanti work in here. I've always wondered if we have some Ashanti ancestry in our family tree. Look at these beautifully ornate tribal masks."

Maya smiled politely and craned her neck to see the photographs. They really were incredible pieces of craftsmanship and art, even to someone like Maya, who wasn't all that interested in history of any kind.

"Look at that sculpture," Morgan said, pointing to the next page. "Their culture had a totally different idea of what was beautiful."

The sculpture showed a female figure with a full, rounded torso and hips.

"The sculptor is showing us that the female form is full and powerful," Mom said. "I like the idea that artists appreciate who we are and what we are. We don't need to look like some little matchstick model in a magazine. We are beautiful and our beauty comes from within."

Maya was fairly certain that she never wanted to look like that sculpture. She was trying to picture those massive hips squeezing into her new green khaki pants. Bad visual. Really bad visual.

"Speaking of models, how's your fashion show shaping up?" Mom asked, pouring dressing on her salad.

Maya could feel Morgan's eyes on her. "Fine," Maya said lightly. "I think everyone has forgiven me for that e-mail mistake. Our first rehearsal went fine. It looks like we're going to have a good show."

"Have all the girls gotten some clothes to wear?" Mom asked.

Maya smiled. "That seems to be working out, too."

"Great," Mom said. "You are a born leader, Maya. You have really taken this whole project and run with it."

"Thanks," Maya said.

After lunch, the three went back to the designer department and looked at some of the most popular labels.

Although most of the clothes were not on sale, Mom agreed to buy three shirts, a dress, and two skirts for Maya. Morgan picked out a light fall jacket and a soft sweater.

"You know how I am about buying clothes," Mom said. "I think it's better to choose a few nice things instead of buying a lot of junk."

Maya smiled. "Hmm. That sounds familiar."

The clerk signaled to Mom. "I'm sorry, ma'am. I'll need to run your card through the scanner again. You know how temperamental these machines can be."

Mom took her credit card out of her wallet again. The clerk ran it through the scanner and handed it back. No one spoke while the machine processed the card.

"I'm so sorry," the clerk said softly. "This says that your card is declined.

chapter.8

"There's got to be some mistake," her mother stated calmly. Maya felt her mouth go dry. She could feel Morgan looking at her. She couldn't bring herself to make eye contact with her sister.

The clerk kept a nervous smile on her face. "It says here that you're over your credit limit."

"That's impossible," Mom said. "I just paid this bill, and I know there are no outstanding charges on this account. And I'm the only person who uses this account."

"Would you like to put these purchases on your Lannings charge account today?" The clerk waited while Mom opened her wallet and pulled out her Lannings charge card.

"I'm sorry," the clerk said, running the Lannings card through the scanner. "These scanners can really get out of whack sometimes. You might want to call your customer service number and get that straightened out."

"Oh, believe me, I will," Mom said in a voice that made Maya shiver.

On the way home, Mom muttered, "If I hadn't *just* paid that bill, I might wonder if there was something else on that charge account. And I know I have a high credit limit on that account. I used that card last spring—to go overseas even. This makes no sense."

Maya listened and nodded. She didn't want to say anything that might prolong the discussion for fear she might blurt out the wrong thing. Her mom was as sharp as a razor blade, and Maya knew her best strategy was silence.

Maya was hanging up her new clothes when she heard Morgan walk into her room and sit on the edge of her bed. Maya didn't turn around.

"You better tell Mom right away what happened," Morgan said.

"I can't do that," Maya said, clipping the price tags off her new jumper. "Not until after the show."

"The show is two weeks away," Morgan insisted. "There's no way you can keep this a secret for two weeks."

Maya turned around to face her sister. "If you'll put even half this effort into helping me with this show, instead of pointing out everything I'm doing wrong, I would appreciate it. Do you want to help me make this a success or not?"

Morgan looked sullen. "How much did you pay for all those outfits you bought online?"

"I honestly don't know," Maya said. "As long as I return everything in two weeks, what difference does it make?"

Morgan wrapped her arms around her stomach and shut her eyes. "This whole thing is giving me a stomach ache. I feel like throwing up."

Maya was disgusted. Every little thing that happened gave Morgan a stomach ache. "Save the barfing for another day," she said. "I thought that our team should take a run this evening when it cools down a little."

"Ugh," Morgan said, rolling into a ball on Maya's bed. "Don't even mention running."

Around 8 P.M. that night, Maya searched the house and back yard for Morgan. But she was nowhere in sight. When Maya telephoned Alex's house, Alex's grandma said the two had gone for a bike ride. *It figures*, Maya thought. *Those two would do anything to get out of a little workout.*

Maya changed into her running clothes and set out for the park. Streetlights bloomed on as she jogged through the dusky evening. Soft lights inside the houses gave each living room the look of a play setting. Maya loved to glance at the windows as she passed and imagine a certain scene unfolding. Some might be comedies, others would be romances. Maya could even imagine a few mysteries being played out in the homes along her jogging route.

By the time she had reached the park, it was dark. But the

lights from the baseball fields and the parking lot kept the summer recreation activities going late into the evening. Maya got a drink from the fountain near the baseball field and was about to jog home when she saw two familiar silhouettes. They were watching a game behind the chain link backstop, and their bikes were propped up against the fence.

Maya sneaked up behind Morgan and Alex.

"Way to look 'em over," Morgan called out. Her friend Jared was at the plate, the bat on his shoulder, waiting for the next pitch. The pitcher threw the ball and Jared's bat connected with a satisfying pop. Morgan and Alex exploded with approval as Jared hot-footed his way to first base.

Maya waited until the noise subsided and then tapped Morgan on the shoulder. Morgan looked around with a smile that disappeared when she saw who was behind her.

"Too sick to work out?" Maya asked sweetly.

"We wanted to see Jared play tonight," Morgan said sheepishly.

"Not that it's any of your business," Alex added before turning her back to Maya.

"We'll see how rude you are tomorrow afternoon when we meet at my house for the weigh-in," Maya said to the back of Alex's head. "Be there around four. That is, if you can remember to keep an appointment."

Without saying goodbye, Maya turned and jogged into the darkness. Why couldn't Alex and Morgan get it through their heads that this was for their own good?

Maya was waiting by the door when the doorbell rang the next morning at 10:15. It was the FedEx lady.

"You can sign here for all of these," she said, pointing to one line on her clipboard of forms.

Maya signed and then took three medium-sized flat boxes. Each one had a different return address.

"Hold on," the courier said when Maya started to close the door. "There's a few more in the truck."

She returned with the other boxes, and Maya brought them inside. Each one was addressed to Maya Cross. She stacked the boxes on top of one another and carefully guided the stack up the stairs to her room.

She opened the package on top. It was wrapped in pale pink tissue with a gold sticker that held the tissue closed. It had obviously come from one of the expensive couture shops online. Maya held her breath and gently peeled the sticker away from the tissue. It was a St. Joseph creation, one that she had selected for herself. The sleeves had tiny gathers with a sweetheart neckline. Maya held the dress in front of her and gazed into the mirror.

"This is so gorgeous," she murmured.

Maya opened the next box. It was from Gazzo—black velvet overalls with funky fake jewels—and it was totally Morgan. Or at least it could be.

The next box contained a full-length skirt with a blue, sequined stretch bodice. "Sweet . . . just wait until Amber sees this," Maya cooed. "She will forget all about her cousin's outfit from J. Crew."

She felt like a movie star, opening box after box of cutting-edge designs. The gown for Bren was perfect with its beaded bodice and full-paneled satin skirt.

There were even ensembles that Jamie and Alex would love. Unable to wait a second longer, Maya logged on the TodaysGirls.com Web site. But no one was in the chat room. So she sent a group e-mail:

Girlfriends--
Just wait till U C the GORGEOUS fashions i have at my house!!!! B here @ 4 p.m. for the group weigh-in and then we can try on all of our fashion slam outfits!
--Maya

Downstairs, on the small bulletin board next to the kitchen telephone, Mom had pinned a $20 bill and a note to Morgan and Maya: "Tonight is staff retreat at Dr. Wettig's house. Order carry-out from Fun Chows. I'll be home @ 10 P.M. Luv U MOM"

Good, Maya told herself. She didn't want her mom to see all the new outfits and wonder where they came from. Mom knew enough about fashion to realize these clothes had not come from the mall.

High-pitched laughter suddenly erupted from the back yard.

Maya looked out the kitchen window and saw Morgan sitting in a circle with three little kids. Another preschooler was walking around the outside of the circle, tapping people's head as she walked past them

"Duck . . . duck . . . duck . . . duck . . . duck . . . *goose!*" One of the kids leaped up and began chasing the other kid around the circle. Everyone was shouting and cheering them on, especially Morgan. *She's such a little kid at heart*, Maya told herself.

Babysitting was something that Maya had always studiously avoided. Sticky hands, runny noses, two million questions. Little kids really got on Maya's nerves. But Morgan loved babysitting and all those things kids did. Unable to contain her enthusiasm about the velvet overalls, Maya impulsively ran outside where Morgan and the kids were playing.

"Hi, guys," Maya said as stood over the circle.

"This is my sister," Morgan told the group. "Her name is Maya."

"She's pretty," said one little girl shyly.

"Thank you," Maya said to the little girl. Maybe little kids weren't so bad after all.

"We're playing while their mommies go to a baby shower," Morgan said.

"No," said a boy who looked to be about three years old. "Babies not take a shower."

"This shower is like a party. It's for a new baby," Morgan said, trying not to grin.

"No. Daddy take a shower," the boy said. "Not a baby."

"That's right," Morgan said. "Babies don't like showers, do they?"

Now Maya remembered why little kids annoyed her. They always had to be right. But Morgan smiled like Mona Lisa, herself—obviously amused but coolly contented.

Later, Maya watched from the kitchen window as the kids' moms thanked Morgan, paid her, and strapped their kids into the various car seat contraptions designed for toddlers. Maya decided it would be a long, long time before she ever got any warm and fuzzy ideas about having children.

At 4 P.M., her friends started arriving for the weigh-in. Bren went first.

"Hey, all right!" Bren said, stepping off the scales. "I'm down two pounds. Break out the banana splits."

Amber went next. "Only one pound?" she said, peering down at the dial.

"A pound is pound, Amber," Bren said. "Don't knock it."

Jamie made everyone close their eyes while she got on the scales. "Okay, you can open your eyes now," Jamie said, beaming. "Almost two pounds."

All the girls looked at Maya.

"Okay, my turn," Maya said stepping onto the scale. "Rats! Only two pounds. I was sure I'd lost at least three pounds."

"It's not good for you to lose too much weight too fast,"

Morgan said. "I read a magazine article about that. That's called yo-yoing and it's really hard on your body."

"Who wants to go first?" Maya said, ignoring Morgan's remark. "Morgan or Alex?"

"This is so stupid," Alex said. "I'm not doing it."

"Come on, Alex," Morgan said. "We've been riding our bikes a lot. Maybe we lost some weight."

Alex rolled her eyes and stepped onto the scale. She immediately stepped off. "Okay," she said to Morgan. "I lost half a pound. Happy?"

"Yeah, that's great," Morgan said, stepping onto the scales and looking down. "Uh-oh. I'm up a pound. My bad."

Maya gave Morgan a disgusted frown.

"I'll lose weight by next week," Morgan said meekly.

"Let's all hope so!" Maya snapped. "You're the only one in the whole group who gained this week. Thanks to you and Miss Thing over there, our team is losing the contest."

Alex exploded. "You may treat your sister like garbage but you're not treating me that way." She grabbed her backpack and glared at Maya. "That's it! I've had it with you, your stupid contest, and this stupid fashion show! I quit!"

Alex stormed out of the room and down the stairs. Everyone stood silently listening as the back door slammed shut.

Morgan looked like she might start crying. "I think I'll go talk to her," she said and hurried out the door.

No one moved in the uneasy silence.

"She never wanted to do this anyway," Maya said with a shrug. "So it goes. Okay. Well, are you guys ready for the fun part? I've got all of our new outfits. We can try them on."

"I don't know," Jamie said, glancing at her watch. "I need to get to work. I'll just try it on later."

Bren stood up. "I need to go, too. Mom and I are eating out with Dad tonight. Mom said to be home as soon as possible."

Maya felt slightly deflated as she watched Jamie and Bren leave. "Maybe we can get together tomorrow," she said as they filed out of the room. "This is going to be a lot of fun."

Maya looked at Amber.

"I guess I'll be going, too," Amber said, picking up her canvas tote bag. "I don't really feel like trying on clothes."

"Just because Alex quit?" Maya asked, her deflation shifting toward disbelief. "She was going to quit anyway. All she ever did was complain."

"No," Amber said. "Not just because Alex quit." She paused for a moment. "You know, Maya, I posted today's Thought for the Day just for you. Did you think about it? At all?"

Maya knew Amber put a lot of effort into writing her Thought for the Day. She couldn't bring herself to tell Amber that she hardly ever read them. But she didn't want her best friend to walk out on her, too.

"I've been so busy with the show," Maya said, "I haven't had a chance to read it yet."

Amber turned and walked out of Maya's room.

Maya sat down at her computer and clicked on TodaysGirls.com. She watched Amber's Thought for the Day window pop open:

It is not fancy hair, gold jewelry, or fine clothes that should make you beautiful. No, your beauty should come from within you—the beauty of a gentle and quiet spirit. This beauty will never disappear, and it is worth very much to God. 1 Peter 3:3–4

Girlfriends, it's not skin goop or eye stuff making you gorgeous, either! It's what's inside—your heart, your soul, your spirit—that makes you for real! Look at other people's inner beauty, not the beauty that disappears, and you'll know how God looks at us! Be real!!

chapter.9

Maya made an appearance in the chat room that night, even though her feelings still stung. Maybe she could cover it up long enough to create a little enthusiasm for the show.

nycbutterfly: so . . . when do U want to try on the dresses?
chicChick: maybe in a couple days?
faithful1: what size did you order 4 me?
nycbutterfly: don't worry about the size. by show time, we will all be skinny enuf to wear them.
chicChick: by show time????? that's less than 2 weeks from now. we won't be different dress sizes in that amount of time. we may need to go to the mall and exchange them for bigger sizes!!!
rembrandt: which store did my dress come from?

Now I am cooked, Maya thought. *I'd better come up with a diversion fast. Real fast.*

> **nycbutterfly:** forget about xchanging the dresses. those
>   were the only sizes i could get.
> **chicChick:** the dresses only come in 1 size??????
> **nycbutterfly:** no, but i didn't have time to bother.

It was getting harder and harder to keep this whole dress-buying thing a secret. And right now Maya had to sign off. Dad's delivery van was in the shop for a few days. He had called Maya earlier and reminded her to pick him up at 9:15 at the restaurant.

> **nycbutterfly:** gotta go pick up dad at gnosh—in a hurry.
>   No worries about the dresses. BBL

Maya was beginning to resent the way everyone was questioning her every decision for this show. She was doing all the work, and no one appreciated it.

She reached for the mouse to click off the chat room, then paused and waited to see who would send the next chat line. Nothing came on the screen for at least twenty seconds. Then a line popped up:

> **faithful1:** is it just me, or is nyc trying to hide something
>   about these dresses?

rembrandt: i think you might b right
jellybean: she just got the dresses in smaller sizes. mayB
   if we try to lose a pound or 2 before the show . . .
faithful1: so she wants us to wear dresses that r 2 small
   for us? nyc is going right over the edge with this.

Maya felt a stabbing pain of betrayal shoot through her stomach. Amber, her best friend, was saying she was over the edge? *How could she say that?*

chicChick: if she yells at jellybean 1 more time . . .
jellybean: she didn't mean 2 hurt my feelings. really. she
   just wants 2 have a great fashion show so she gets a
   little bossy.
rembrandt: a LITTLE bossy? i would hate 2 C a LOT bossy!!!

Maya read the screen in disbelief. All of her so-called friends were raking her over the coals—right in front of her eyes!

faithful1: nyc has no right 2 treat you that way, jb. it
   makes me furious!!!
chicChick: this fashion show is a big pain. my parents
   said I could bring everybody 2 the lake this weekend
   to stay 4 a whole week! r u guys up for it?
faithful1: sounds great!
rembrandt: if i can get off work YES!

chicChick: YAY!! Can be our last gasp before classes start

jellybean: maybe we all need to get away 4 a few days.
    just have fun 2gether!

faithful1: maybe some fresh air will bring maya back to
    her senses.

Maya glanced down at her watch—9:20 P.M. At least she thought it said 9:20. She could barely read her watch for the tears in her eyes. *Back to my senses? How can they criticize me like this? I'm the only one acting sensibly!!*

Maya left the chat room still running on her computer. She grabbed her keys and headed downstairs. Morgan was sitting at the kitchen breakfast bar, typing on the laptop. She looked up from the screen, and their eyes met.

Maya could tell that Morgan saw her tears. She brushed past Morgan and strode out into the night with an air of wounded dignity. Talk behind her back, would they?

Maya's dad was waiting out in front of the Gnosh by the time she arrived.

"Sorry I'm late," Maya said, throwing the car into first gear and pulling back into traffic.

Dad leaned his head back against the headrest. "What a day. That soft drink machine is more trouble! So what did you make for dinner? I never did take any time to eat this evening."

Maya had to stop and remember what they had eaten for

dinner. "Take out Chinese. There's plenty left. Jacob ate dinner at Ryan's house, so we actually have leftovers."

Dad laughed. "And how is my fashion show producer?"

"I'm just fine," she said grimly. "No thanks to my back-stabbing friends who are telling each other that I've gone over the edge."

Mr. Cross shook his head. "Trouble in paradise, huh? What's up?"

"I'm doing all the work," Maya said. "I pick the clothes, I arrange the rehearsals, I try to get everyone to watch their weight. And all they can do is complain about it. The only person who defended me was Morgan."

Her dad smiled. "Yeah, that Morgan is alright. She is one loyal sister."

"And now they're all talking about going to Bren's cabin for the week," Maya grumbled.

"Sounds like fun," Dad said. "An end-of-summer getaway just for your friends. You and Morgan ought to go."

Maya looked at her dad incredulously. "I can't be running off to Bren's cabin for a whole week. I have a fashion show to organize. By myself."

Maya parked Mr. Beep in their driveway and turned off the engine.

"You know, Maya," her dad said slowly. "If you want the other girls to help you with this, you could always let them make some of the decisions."

Maya shook her head. "Every time I do that, they mess it up.

You should see what they wanted to wear in this show. It was so small-town and pathetic."

Mr. Cross shrugged. "Edgewood is a small town. There's nothing wrong with that. We moved out here so you kids could enjoy it—the closeness and safety—it helps you grow long-term values. Enjoy your small-town life and your small-town friends. These high school years go by way too fast. Don't waste a minute of them squabbling over something as fickle and short-lived as fashion, Maya."

"Yeah, I guess," Maya said without enthusiasm.

"You guess?" her dad said playfully. "You know I'm always right!"

Maya laughed wearily. "At least I know where I get my attitude."

They got out of the car and went in the house. Maya found Morgan in her bedroom, scratching her cat's head. Vinnie had been a stray and was half-starved when Morgan found him. Now he was a rotund, orange tabby who spent most of the day snoozing on Morgan's bed.

"Thanks for defending me," Maya said.

Morgan smiled. "They didn't mean anything by it. If they knew what was really going on, they wouldn't be trying to get you to switch the dress sizes."

"I can't tell anyone about that except you," Maya said. "This has got to stay our secret."

Morgan looked troubled. "Why don't we all go up to Bren's

cabin and just have fun? We'll be back in plenty of time for the show."

"Absolutely not," Maya said. "Those guys don't care about this show at all. They won't exercise or eat right up at the cabin. You know how it is when we go there. Bren's parents let us order subs and pizzas and fried chicken and every other greasy thing on Earth. It's a week-long food-fest. And you know those dresses aren't getting any bigger."

Morgan held Vinnie in her arms like a fat, furry baby. "I really want to go to the cabin."

"Then go," Maya said. "If you would rather go up there and stuff your face every night, you go right ahead."

Morgan winced. "That's not why I want to go! I want to go have fun one more time before school starts. I'm not like you, Maya. I don't care if I have the perfect 'magazine' body. I just want to look like me."

Maya walked to the door of Morgan's bedroom. "You know, even if you don't care what you look like, I do. And believe me, someone needs to care how you look."

chapter.10

Twenty and up . . . and down. Twenty one and up . . . and down. Twenty two—"

Maya was holding Morgan's feet to the floor while Morgan struggled to finish her twenty five sit-ups. After the exercises, Maya planned for them to take a jog to the park and back.

"Can't we wait until it's dark?" Morgan gasped. "Running during the daytime makes me light-headed."

"We're not running, we're jogging," Maya corrected. "Sure, we can run after the sun goes down. At least I know you won't go sneaking off to the ballpark or Alex's house this time."

Not with Alex and her other deadbeat friends lounging around at Bren's cabin all week. They had all packed up and gotten out of town fast. Although they'd assured Maya they would be back for rehearsal on Friday, Maya was furious. The fashion show and mixer were on Saturday, just one day after they got back. *If just one of them gets sunburned, sprains an ankle, or catches poison ivy, then everything will be ruined,* she thought in terror.

"Let's check in and see what they're up to," Morgan said after finishing her last sit-up. She went to Maya's computer and logged on while Maya did her make-up. Before they left, the girls had agreed to contact Maya and Morgan around lunchtime.

Morgan typed in her ID name and password. The screen flashed, Welcome to Today'sGirls.com, and Amber's Thought for The Day opened itself.

"I like to read these," Morgan said. "They always make me think."

Morgan read aloud: "'I will praise you because you made me in an amazing and wonderful way.' Psalms 139:14 How could our human hands improve on 'amazing and wonderful' at the divine level? God's already got us covered! This means the only thing we can really change or improve is what's inside. We already know which one is our real job to improve."

"So in other words, that gives everyone the right to pig out on junk food all week," Maya said sarcastically.

"No," Morgan said. "All Amber is saying is that inner beauty is more important."

"Sounds to me like they found a convenient excuse to eat their weight in potato chips," Maya replied.

Morgan signed into the chat room, and Maya read over her shoulder.

jellybean: hi campers! whuzzup?
TX2step: last nite, when we were on the dock, we heard an owl hooting in the forest. it was so kewl!!!!

"They heard a owl hooting last night," Morgan said.

"Isn't that special?" Maya answered. "Were they out on a night hike?"

Morgan typed in the question, and they waited for the response.

"Nope," Morgan said. "Alex said they were sitting on the screened porch."

"Eating potato chips?" Maya asked.

Morgan ignored the comment and typed.

jellybean: what are u guys doing 2day?
TX2step: swimming in the lake, then building a campfire 2nite. roasting hot dogs 4 dinner, marshmallows 4 dessert. Bren's mom got chocolate bars and graham crackers so we are making s'mores mmmmmmm . . .

Morgan groaned. "They're making s'mores! S'mores are my favorite food in the entire world."

"Terrific," Maya grumbled. "They're gonna turn into little butterballs."

jellybean: i am so jealous!!!!!! eat a smore 4 me!
TX2step: i will. in fact i may eat 20 of them!

"I think I'll ask them what they had for lunch."

"What is this?" Maya shrieked. "A food review? Or don't they do anything else up there besides eat?" She stalked to the makeup mirror to scrutinize and touch up her lips.

Morgan smiled ruefully. "I wish we were up there, having fun with them. Especially since Dad gave Jamie the time off and told us to go with them. We should have gone. I feel left out."

Maya finished applying raspberry lip gloss and snapped the container closed. "I told you to go with them. But you wouldn't go unless I did. And there was no way I was going up there and watch them eat themselves into oblivion."

Maya stood up and patted her hair into place. "Forget those guys for awhile. I've got an idea. Why don't you call Jared and tell him we'll be at the pool in a half hour? We can just hang out there until dinner and then go jogging tonight, like you wanted anyway."

Morgan grinned. "Cool. I hope he hasn't gone somewhere."

Jared was at home and agreed to meet Morgan at the pool. The girls grabbed their pool passes and towels and drove to the pool. Mr. Beep was sputtering a little, and Maya worried that he might not make it all the way to the pool without stalling out. After adding up her recent earnings from the Gnosh, Maya knew she had almost enough money to go used car shopping with her dad.

"Mr. Beep needs a tune-up," Maya told Morgan. "But I don't want to waste my savings on plugs, points, filters, and oil. Lazy old car," she muttered, as he choked and wheezed to a stop in the parking lot.

Jared was waiting for Morgan by the main entrance. Although the day was sunny and warm, there were only a few people at the pool. The grassy lawn that had been crowded with sunbathers all summer long now seemed empty and forlorn. *Bren would be completely depressed to see this*, Maya thought.

Out of habit, Maya spread her towel near the pine trees where her friends always gathered. She lay down, put on her sunglasses, and flipped through the new issue of *Cool* magazine. There were the usual ads: cute, skinny girls in cool clothes, grinning happily without a care in the world. Obviously, none of them were trying to stage a fashion show in the next week.

Maya browsed through "Is It Infatuation or Love? 20 Questions That Give You the Answer!" She pondered question number 5: "When you haven't seen him all day long, then suddenly he appears, walking toward you, smiling . . . Do you think:

A. What great biceps.

B. He looks great in that outfit.

C. Now we can finish that conversation.

D. I hope he doesn't see this zit on my nose."

"Hello."

Maya looked up and saw Greg Muir, towering overhead. Even with her sunglasses on, she had to shade her eyes to see his face.

"Hi," Maya said, casually noticing his perfect biceps. "I didn't know you were here." She flushed suddenly, remembering the magazine question.

Greg knelt down on the grass next to her. "Yeah. I never know what to do with the last couple days before school starts. You know, it's kind of boring."

Maya smiled, hoping he didn't notice her reddening cheeks. "Yeah, I know what you mean. Everybody else went up to Bren's cabin this week. But I thought I should stay here and work on the fashion show. Are you coming to the rehearsal on Friday afternoon?"

"Oh yeah, I'll be there," Greg said. "Hey, I hope you aren't mad about Brandon and me goofing around at practice. "

Maya laughed effortlessly. "Oh no. Everyone was being silly that day. No problem."

"Good," Greg said. "Well, I guess I'll go do some laps. I'll see you Friday then."

Maya smiled. "See ya."

As she watched Greg walk away, Maya could hardly restrain herself from squealing "Yes!" But she quickly remembered that nobody else was around to share her joy. Morgan was off somewhere with Jared. Bren, Amber, and Jamie were miles and miles away, having a good time without her.

She tried to read her magazine. But Maya kept thinking of what she and Morgan were going to miss tonight: a circle of good friends around the campfire, hanging out under a starlit sky. Maya loved the soothing night sounds of the forest, feeling safe within the bright ring of a campfire's glow.

Turning back to the magazine, Maya started reading one of the feature articles. It was a girl's personal account of dieting titled, "I Wanted To Never Eat Again." This girl had starved herself to the point where she was admitted to a hospital, and the doctors threatened to feed her with a tube. Looking at the girl's photo gave Maya a sick feeling, and she had to close the magazine and take a deep breath.

After her head cleared, she looked at her watch. It was only 4 o'clock, and they didn't need to be home until five. But Maya felt restless and bored, so she walked off to find Morgan.

Maya surveyed the area around the pool. But Morgan was nowhere near the pool. She checked the dressing rooms, but Morgan wasn't in there either. Next she padded around the refreshment stand and saw Greg and Brandon sitting on top of one of the picnic tables, eating frozen Snickers. Greg waved and Maya walked toward them. Now that she'd realized she only liked Greg when Brandon wasn't around, she felt eager to get away from them as soon as possible.

"I was just leaving," she said to Greg. "But I need to give my sister a ride home. And I don't see her anywhere."

Greg and Brandon gave each other a conspiratorial look.

"Better check around that corner," Brandon said, pointing back over his shoulder to the snack bar. "We saw her go back there with that tubby dude. They were carrying a plate of chili fries that would give you a hernia!"

As if she were in a bad dream, Maya walked away from the boys and around the corner. Sitting on the grass and leaning up against the concrete wall, Morgan and Jared were lifting long French fries out of a puddle of chili sauce and shredded cheese. They dangled the fries over their faces before lowering the long gooey strands into their open mouths. They looked like two big baby birds in a nest, taking worms from an invisible mother.

Maya gasped and Morgan looked up in horror. In one motion, Morgan flung the chili fry from her fingertips—aiming toward the grass. Instead, it landed with a wet slap, wrapping itself around Maya's leg—just below her left knee. Morgan stood up, wiping her gooey fingers on her tank suit.

"I'm, I'm sorry," Morgan said.

Maya was rigid with fury. She turned and stomped away, her eyes blazing. She returned to the lawn, gathered her towel and tote, and marched to the car. By that time, Morgan had grabbed her things and was trotting several paces behind Maya.

Cranking the ignition, Mr. Beep came to life in a roar. Morgan opened the car door and leaped in just as Maya was throwing the car in reverse. They jerked backwards, then forwards, the tires spitting gravel as they raced to the street.

Maya navigated her way through traffic in silence. Morgan

kept quiet, clutching the handle above the door as the little car jerked to a stop at intersections and then took off again. They pulled up the driveway to the garage, and Maya jammed the vehicle to a sudden stop. She turned off the ignition and took out the keys.

"I give up on you," she said in an icy voice. "No more hiding behind the snack bar. From now on, you do what you want. Just leave me out of it."

Maya got out of the car and stomped into the house. She went up to her room and turned on her computer. Calling up the e-mail program, she typed in a message to Bren's address. It read:

Happy Campers--

Be advised that everyone is still required to eat healthy, low-fat food and exercise regularly. At Friday's rehearsal, anyone who does not fit into her assigned outfit will be immediately cut from the show. There will be no exceptions.

--Maya

Listen up, people!" Maya's voice echoed off the gym walls. It was Friday afternoon and she was reading a list of announcements from her clipboard.

"First we do a run-through of the runway walking order. Then I'll distribute the outfits, and you can try them on in the locker rooms. Please be very careful with these clothes. They must be returned undamaged. Understand?"

Everyone nodded. Greg and Brandon were their usual clowning selves, elbowing and whispering comments to each other. The cheerleaders were listening attentively, perky as ever. Amber, Jamie, and Morgan were sitting quietly off to one side. When they had arrived at the gym with Bren, they all seemed detached, saying nothing about their week at the cabin.

Maya had retreated into preparing her script for the show

and browsing the Web sites that offered an endless array of international designer clothes.

"One other thing," Maya continued. "I'm going to need everyone's help tomorrow morning, setting up the runway and the PA system. Can I count on everybody to be here around 10 A.M.?"

Heads were nodding again.

"Great," Maya said. "O.K. Let's get started."

Maya pressed the play button on the stereo. The bass notes pumped out a disco beat, and everyone came forward to their spot in the line. This time, the students seemed more interested in getting through their trips down the runway than in making the others laugh.

When all the models had done their walks and returned to the line, Maya turned off the stereo. "That was excellent," she said. "Now be patient while I get the clothes passed out. And remember, when you try them on, be very careful. Keep the necklines and collars *off* your makeup, and clean up *first* if you're sweaty."

She gave Greg and Brandon their outfits. "Try these on and then change back into your own clothes. I'll take them home with me and steam out any wrinkles for the show."

Maya had borrowed Dad's van and hung a shower curtain bar across the back to transport the fashions to and from the show. She called out the names of the cheerleaders, handing them their clothes on hangers. Then she called out Jamie, Alex, and Morgan to pick up theirs. All the girls disappeared into the locker room.

Maya stayed in the gym to wait for Brandon and Greg.

In less than five minutes, the guys were strolling across the gym. *I definitely picked the right guys for this job,* Maya thought as she watched them saunter toward her. Both guys wore their clothes with the casual elegance of magazine models.

"Whaddaya think?" Greg said, holding out his arms and turning left and right.

"You guys look great," Maya said, smiling.

"Yeah," Brandon said jokingly. "We know!"

Maya pretended to be annoyed.

"Okay, you two!" Maya said with mock disapproval. "I'll take those clothes back right now!"

The guys laughed and headed back to the locker room. By then, most of the cheerleaders had come back out with their clothes on the hangers.

"These clothes look so cool!" Meg bubbled. "We are going to look so totally awesome!"

Maya smiled. "Just hang them up on this rack, and I'll take them home tonight. See you tomorrow at ten."

The cheerleaders left and the gym fell silent again. There was no sign of her friends. Maya decided to go see what was happening in the locker room.

As she pushed open the door, she heard Bren's voice. "I don't know. This is so messed up."

Maya walked into the changing area. Morgan was sitting on a bench with her head slumped over and her eyes closed.

"Morgan's dizzy," Bren said. "She almost fainted just now. Something is wrong."

Maya gave Morgan a skeptical glance. "What's wrong, Morgan?"

"Nothing," she said, opening her eyes and smiling weakly. "I must have stood up too fast."

Bren shook her head. "It was more than that, Morgan. You nearly passed out a minute ago."

Morgan smiled. "I think I just stumbled over this bench. I'm fine now."

"Good, you had me worried there," Maya said, looking around the locker room. "So how are the dresses?"

Amber had her dress on but unzipped at the back. "I really wish you had ordered these in our correct sizes, Maya. I'm afraid to zip this up. It's way too tight. If I force this zipper up and break it, then the dress is damaged."

Jamie was sitting in her dress, looking glum. "Same here, Maya. These dresses are gorgeous. But they are the wrong size. I can't get my zipper up either."

From the look on Bren's face, Maya knew her dress didn't fit either.

"Okay, maybe I should have asked your sizes," Maya said. "But you guys didn't help matters by stuffing your faces at the lake all week. And sitting on your butts instead of exercising. Why is it that all the cheerleaders fit into their outfits? Except Bren??"

"Probably because you got their right sizes!" Bren snapped. "Why is it that you could figure out the right sizes for them, but you couldn't for us?"

Maya was stung by Bren's retort. "Oh, yeah, that's right! I like them a whole lot better than you guys! Or maybe it was because they didn't use this week for an eat-a-thon!"

Amber held up her hands for quiet. "Hold on. Let's keep it together here. Maya, we're all pretty sick of hearing what pigs we are because we went to the lake and ate the same food we always do. And when you go to the lake, you eat the same food as we do. You have seriously gone overboard with this eating thing."

"Why can't we just wear the clothes we tried on at Bren's that night?" Jamie asked. "If we wear our own clothes, we won't look so ridiculous."

Maya was fuming. "Ridiculous? You think you look ridiculous in clothes by New York designers? The cheerleaders didn't think they looked ridiculous. They thought they looked cool. I think it's a pretty sad day when the cheerleaders have better taste than you do!"

Amber stood up and began taking off her dress. "I think it's a pretty sad day when you insult your friends and pick on your sister about some idiotic fashion show. I have had it. I love you like a sister, Maya, but you need to get your head on straight. Until you do, I quit."

"Me, too," said Jamie, taking off her dress. "This has gotten so nasty, I don't want any part of it."

Maya was furious. "You can't just walk out of here! What am I supposed to do for models?

Bren was taking off her dress. She stopped and grabbed the

handle of a push broom that was leaning against the wall. "Here, use this," she said. "This is the only thing that will fit in my dress."

Maya watched with a scowl as they hung their dresses on hangers and put the hangers on a wardrobe bar. "Don't expect me to come begging for you to be in the show."

Amber looked at her friend. "I don't expect that," she said sadly. "I know you too well."

The girls walked out of the locker room, and the door slowly sighed shut behind them. Maya looked at Morgan, and Morgan shook her head.

"How did things get this messed up?" Morgan said softly.

Maya gave Morgan a perturbed look. "Come on. Let's get these clothes into Dad's van. I don't have time for a bunch of whiners who want me to baby them every inch of the way. We'll do this show without them."

The sisters hauled all the dresses to the van, hung them up carefully, and then drove home. As Maya pulled the van into the driveway, she noticed her mother sitting on a chaise lounge in the backyard. She walked up as the girls got out of the van. Before they could say anything, Mom opened the back door and surveyed the glittering array of fashions hanging on the bar.

"That would explain this," Mom said coldly, waving a piece of paper in her hand. "Now I would like to hear how this happened. And this time, make it the truth."

Maya took the paper and looked at it. The credit card company had faxed a list of all the charges on her mother's credit card. At the bottom, the charges were totaled: $6,529. Maya gasped.

"Do you mean to tell me that you didn't even know how much you were paying for all of these clothes?" Mom asked.

Maya shook her head. "I was going to return them. After the show."

"You are returning these clothes today," her mother said quietly. "The fashion show is canceled."

chapter.12

After a long level-headed discussion and plenty of apologetic tears from Maya, Mom said the show could go on.

"Canceling the show wouldn't be fair to all the other kids," Mom said. "But all the clothes are going back. Today."

That proved to be more of a problem than Maya had thought it would be. When she called to get instructions for returning the clothes, several online stores said they did not accept returns. So Maya couldn't send back the pieces she had ordered for Greg, Brandon, Meg, or Morgan.

"Looks like you bought yourself four outfits," Mom said.

When Maya added up the cost of those four outfits and the return postage for all of the other outfits, the total came to $870. That all but wiped out her car fund of $990.

"You still have $120," Mom said. "It's a start."

"I think I better spend that on Mr. Beep," Maya said. "Or I'll be walking to school."

After carefully folding and boxing all the outfits that she could return, Maya called Meg and told her about the other cheerleaders' outfits.

"But I still get to wear mine?" Meg squealed, obviously thrilled at her good fortune.

"Yeah," Maya said, "if you'll agree to call all the other cheer-leaders and tell them they need to find something to wear for tomorrow night."

Morgan wandered in later and offered to wear something old, since Maya no longer had a designer outfit to wear.

"Don't be silly," Maya said gently. "If you can fit into your outfit, you deserve to wear it. But thanks."

The next morning at 10 A.M., Maya and Morgan were stand-ing in the empty gym. The platforms for the runway were stacked neatly where the janitors had left them.

"Where is everybody?" Maya asked, her voice echoing in the gym.

Morgan shrugged.

"Hi!" a voice said from the far end of the gym. Jared waved and joined them.

"Morgan said you might need some help setting up for the show," Jared said.

"We sure do!" Maya said. "Thanks for coming."

The three of them set to work, carrying and setting up the

platforms. Before long, Brandon and Greg sauntered into the gym.

"Glad you could make it," Maya said. "Why don't you guys set up the podium and the speakers for the announcer."

"Okay," Brandon said, grabbing a basketball and shooting a hoop. Greg grabbed the ball and took a shot. Maya stood up and watched Brandon take the ball for another shot.

"Hey," Maya said. "We need some help. Either set up platforms with us, or do the speaker system."

"We'll do the speakers," Brandon said, eyeing up his next shot at the basket. "In a minute."

Just then, Meg and several other cheerleaders bounded into the gym.

"We want to take a shot," Meg shrieked and ran over to Brandon and Greg.

"Better watch it," Brandon said aloud and then whispered something into Meg's ear. Meg turned, looked at Maya, and giggled. Brandon started dribbling the ball around Meg as if she were a player on the other team. Meg was convulsed with a torrent of giggles.

"Forget them," Jared said. "We've done most of this ourselves anyway."

Maya nodded wearily. "I really appreciate your help."

"No problem," Jared said, smiling shyly at Morgan. "I'm looking forward to watching this show tonight."

After more dribbling, Brandon and Greg carried the speakers to the end of the runway and connected the microphone to the amplifier.

"Testing, testing. One, two, three," Brandon said into the mike. "Would all the mega-babes please report to the podium as soon as possible . . ."

This sent the cheerleaders into new paroxysms of laughter. Maya, Morgan, and Jared carried the last platform to the end of the runway, folded down the legs, and secured the crossbars. Then all three of them sat down on the platform for a welcomed rest.

"Jared and I are going to the Gnosh for a Diet Coke," Morgan said. "Wanna come?"

Maya shook her head. "You guys go ahead," she said. "I've got to take care of a few things here. And then I need to thank the comedians over there for all of their generous help today. You know, it really makes me wonder about something."

Jared smiled. "What's that?"

"I wonder why those two bothered to build up all of their muscles when the only ones they ever use are in their jaws."

"That is a good question," Jared said. " Oh, well. See you at the show tonight."

Morgan and Jared were gone before Maya strolled over to the group. "Got that microphone working?" she asked evenly of Brandon.

"Yeah," Brandon replied, giving her a flirty grin. "Want to sing me a love song?"

"Not exactly," Maya said, turning her back on him to face

the cheerleaders with the mike. "Listen, for those of you who will be wearing your own clothes tonight, come early so I can write a description of your outfit for my notecards. Be here around 6:30. Any questions?"

Meg stuck up her hand. "I think I'll buy some new high-heeled shoes this afternoon to go with my new outfit. Don't you think that it would look totally awesome?"

Maya felt like she was listening to Meg's voice through a long tunnel. "Yeah, Meg," Maya murmured. "Awesome."

Maya walked out to the parking lot and climbed into Mr. Beep. Instead of going straight home, she decided to ship the boxes of clothes back to the online stores. Just looking at that stack of boxes made her feel foolish. The sooner those things were out of the back seat, the better.

The post office was closed, but Maya found a QuickShip store that was still open. She hauled the boxes inside and then wrote a $45 check for the shipping cost. It felt just like watching a stack of dollar bills fly out of her hands.

Maya got back in Mr. Beep and was about to head home when she remembered Morgan and Jared had gone to the Gnosh Pit. They had set up those platforms, working all morning like fry-cooks with three church buses in the parking lot. Maya felt a sudden surge of love for her sister and that stubborn streak of loyalty of hers. Maya decided to drive by and give both of them a ride home just to show her appreciation.

Maya turned and headed toward her dad's restaurant. She parked in back and walked in through the kitchen door entrance. As she neared the serving window, Maya could hear laughter. Amber's laughter. And Bren's voice. And Jamie's voice, mixed with Morgan's and Jared's. All sharing a funny story.

"So we're sitting on the porch, and Amber sees this raccoon out in the dark," Bren was saying between peals of laughter. "And my mom and dad had just finished telling us about all the timber wolves in the woods up there and how their eyes shine red in the dark. So Amber gets one look at this raccoon, with its eyes glowing like red light bulbs right back at her, and she screams and we all go . . ."

The group erupted with laughter and squeals at the horrified face Bren was probably making right now. And Maya realized that she had never felt more alone and lost from her friends than she did at this very moment. There was no way that she could walk through that door and pull up a chair and join in the laughter and silliness.

Maya felt a sob rising in her throat. She swallowed and tried to choke her sadness back. She turned and walked quietly out the back of the restaurant. She got into her car and turned over the ignition. Mr. Beep rumbled to a start, and Maya took the back exit of the parking lot, so no one could see her driving away.

chapter.13

By the time Morgan had returned from the Gnosh, Maya had showered, dressed, done her hair and make-up, and was finishing a second coat of nail polish.

Without her beautiful designer outfit, Maya had two choices. She could either wear the pale blue, cap-sleeved, empire-waist dress she had worn to last year's spring dance. Or she could wear the pink satin dress with a sweetheart neck and spaghetti straps she had gotten for her birthday.

Usually, on the night of the back-to-school mixer, there would be a flurry of phone calls and e-mails to and from the Cross household. Bren could never decide which dress to wear. Amber usually wanted advice on wearing her hair up or down. And Jamie always needed a ride. At some point, Mr. Cross would make some wry comment to his daughters about how

"General Schwartzkopf hadn't put this much effort into planning Operation Desert Storm."

But tonight the phone was silent. Maya hadn't even turned on her computer. She wanted so badly to talk to her friends right now—only she knew that they didn't want to talk with her.

So, all alone, Maya chose the pink satin dress. But before she put it on, she stepped on the scales. The needle dutifully moved to 115 pounds. Even yesterday, that reading would have made her jump for joy. But today, it was just one more empty triumph. After zipping herself into the dress, Maya poked her head into Morgan's bedroom. "Hey," Maya said. "As soon as you're ready, I'll do your hair and make-up." Morgan was sitting on her bed. "Great," she said, her voice tired. "Just let me get a quick shower first." Maya was struck by Morgan's lack of enthusiasm. "You seem kind of draggy. Do you need a fifteen-minute beauty nap?"

Morgan was famous for her catnapping. She could sleep almost anywhere—in the car, on a lawn chair in the back yard—and wake up perky. But this evening, Morgan just shook her head. "I'll be fine. I just need a shower to get me going."

As Maya listened to the shower spray, she thought about the last three weeks and all the times that Morgan had stuck by her. She truly was the world's best sister. And tonight, Maya decided, she would show Morgan just how much she appreciated her.

After Morgan put on her designer velvet overalls with the lace-edged white cotton tee-shirt and the cool jeweled buttons and clasps, Maya had her turn around.

"You look fantastic," Maya said. "I've never seen you look more thin and sophisticated."

Morgan grinned. "Thanks, Maya. Are you ready to give me the full beauty makeover?"

Maya made a sweeping bow toward her bedroom. "If you will please step into my salon, mademoiselle?"

Morgan led the way to Maya's room and sat down at her well-stocked makeup table. After pulling Morgan's shoulder-length hair up into a jeweled clip, Maya styled her bangs and ponytail into a series of soft twirls. It gave Morgan the look of a country-clubbing college girl, who probably drove a fancy sports car.

Next Maya applied a light dusting of French vanilla shadow over Morgan's eyelids and curled her top lashes. After touching her top and bottom lashes with black mascara, Maya used a little blush on her cheeks for a fresh dewy look. And to stay with a casual color scheme, she applied a raspberry jam gloss on Morgan's lips.

"Say," Maya teased. "Is that my baby sister or a rising young movie star?"

When the girls walked downstairs, their parents were in the kitchen, sitting at the breakfast bar.

"My goodness, Dr. Cross!" their dad said." You certainly have two lovely daughters. Please allow me to take their photographs."

The girls stood together while their dad snapped off a few

shots. Then he insisted that his wife pose with the girls. Mom stood in the middle and the three of them grinned into the lens.

"For what it's worth, Maya," her mom said, "I never saw you in that designer outfit. But I know that you could never look any prettier than you do in this dress."

Maya hugged her mom. "Thanks."

The telephone rang and both girls turned to answer it. But Maya jerked her hand away from the receiver at the last second. "You go ahead, Morgan," she said sheepishly. "It might be Jared."

Morgan answered the telephone. "Hello? No, it isn't. No problem. Bye."

Morgan hung up the phone. "Wrong number," both girls said to each other at the same time and laughed.

"Could you two young ladies use a chauffeur this evening?" Mr. Cross asked with a slight bow.

"No thanks, Dad," Maya said. "Mr. Beep's driving."

Even Jacob came out of the family room and whistled appreciatively. "You two look really great," he said.

"Aren't you coming to the mixer?" Morgan asked.

"I'll be up there later on with Ryan," Jacob assured her. "I just don't need to be the first one there. I didn't organize this thing like you guys did. Good luck."

Maya smiled. *I'll need it,* she thought.

Mr. Beep puttered into the parking lot and wheezed as Maya turned off the ignition. She patted the tiny dashboard. "Thanks for getting me here," she said aloud. "You're getting a complete tune-up next week. Don't give out on me just yet."

The girls walked across the parking lot and through the front doors of the school. From down the hall came a long, low wolf whistle.

"Looking good," said Kevin Comes, Maya's lab partner from last year's biology class.

"Thanks," Maya said coyly. "Have you seen Mr. Carson? He's supposed to be here somewhere."

"I saw him about ten minutes ago in the gym," Kevin said. "He's probably still there."

The girls walked into the gym. Mr. Carson was helping one of the drama club technicians set up a roving spotlight.

"This just arrived yesterday," Mr. Carson said. "We bought it with the profits from the drama club's spring musical. Would you like to use it tonight? Jeremy here can run it for you. I just showed him how it works."

"Thank you so much," Maya said, turning on the charm. "Do you mind, Jeremy? You could give our show a real professional touch." Jeremy just nodded, blushing.

Mr. Carson stopped and scratched his chin. "You know, Maya, when you first suggested this show, I had some real reservations about doing it. I thought it might create some rivalries and arguments between the students. But I'm impressed with the way you organized it and made it happen. Congratulations."

Maya couldn't allow herself to think of how badly she had

handled almost every aspect of the show. She needed to keep it together enough to see the evening through to some sort of conclusion. At this point, it wouldn't serve any purpose to confess the entire litany of mistakes she had made to Mr. Carson. But she did want to saying something that was true.

"One thing I can honestly say," Maya said. "I've learned quite a bit from this experience."

Mr. Carson smiled. "That's what leadership is all about, Maya. Learning how to do it better the next time."

"In that case," Maya said, "I might just qualify as a pro!"

Meg bounded up to where Maya and Mr. Carson were standing. As they had been instructed to do, Meg and the other cheerleaders arrived early so that Maya could make her notes.

"You guys look so totally beautiful tonight," Meg said to Morgan and Maya. "This is such a cool way to start the school year. I am so glad you thought of this, Maya."

Meg was being sincere and genuinely sweet this evening. But all these wonderful compliments felt like they should be going to someone else. *How could I make so many mistakes and get this many strokes for the same event?* Maya wondered.

"You look really nice tonight too, Meg," Maya said. "That color goes great with your complexion."

Meg clutched her hands to her chest. "Well, you picked out this dress. So I owe it all to you. I told my mom that you were giving me this dress because the store didn't accept returns. And she insists that we pay you for this dress."

"That's fine," Maya said. "My parents said that any money I get for these clothes will go to charity. So just give it to the Humane Society."

Students were beginning to gather in the gym. From the corner of her eye, Maya saw Bren, Amber, and Jamie walk into the gym together.

Jamie was wearing Levi straight-legs and a new Nike baseball shirt. Bren had the wheat-colored jean skirt and striped top she had worn that night at her house. Amber had on her favorite chinos and a square-necked, short-sleeved cotton sweater.

They all look great, just the way they are, Maya thought. But from where they stood over by the door, they felt so far away, so out of reach. They might as well have been standing on the other side of the Grand Canyon.

Maya heard the band warming up as she finished writing the notes on her index cards. She told the cheerleaders to meet her by the podium no later than 8:15. Maya glanced at the clock in the hall. It was shortly after 7:30 and the fashion show was supposed to start in less than an hour.

As the minutes ticked away, Maya grew more jittery. After she did a final sound check, she would be ready to go find Morgan for some sisterly moral support.

The gym was filling with students. Maya and Jeremy worked out a few hand and vocal cues for the roving spotlight.

"This is going to be too cool," Jeremy said. "I'll see you back here at 8:15."

Maya nodded, feeling the pre-show nerves take hold of her. It had been at least a half hour since she had seen Morgan.

Something seemed strange about her sister tonight. But Maya had been too preoccupied by the show preparations to pay close attention. *Besides,* she told herself, *everything seems strange tonight.*

She searched in both of the girls' restrooms and in the outside hallway. No Morgan. An inescapable panic coursed through Maya's veins. She felt like a toddler lost in a large department store. Hands shaking, she scanned the crowd for Jared. He would know where Morgan was.

At the end of the runway, she saw Brandon and Greg doing muscle poses in their fashion show clothes for a group of girls. She hurried toward them, her satin dress making swishing noises as she jostled her way through the crowd.

"Greg!" she shouted over the band's music, grabbing his arm. "Have you seen my sister? Or my sister's friend from the pool the other day?"

Greg grinned. "Chill, Maya. You look like you're ready to blow a fuse. No, I haven't seen your sister at all tonight. Or her friend, what's-his-name. Brandon," he nudged his friend. "Have you seen Maya's sister anywhere? Or that guy she hangs around with? You know, Tubby—"

"His name is Jared!" Maya exploded at Greg. "Not Tubby! He has a name! His name is Jared!"

"Hey, excuse me," Greg sneered. "I'm sorry that I don't know every twerp in this school by name."

"You know, it's not like you're some kind of big humanitarian," Brandon added quickly. "You've been looking down your nose at him all summer, too. Remember?"

Maya walked away, too stunned to think of a comeback. She felt as if she had been slapped—with the truth. And it stung. If her attitude toward Jared had been that obvious to Brandon and Greg, then Morgan had to know it, too.

She walked toward the stage, and there was Jared, bopping to the music. She rushed up to him, grabbed his arm, and shouted, "Have you seen Morgan?"

Jared smiled. "Yeah," he shouted over the music. "By the refreshment table! About twenty minutes ago!"

The gym was getting warmer and noisier.

"And now, students," Mr. Carson was saying into the microphone. "Our back-to-school fashion show will be held in the middle of the gymnasium. Please find a good viewing spot on either side of our runway. Thank you."

Maya checked her watch. Here she was, at the weight she wanted to be, with the fashion show finally ready to go. And she felt completely and utterly miserable. Where was Morgan?

The cheerleaders were waiting behind Maya, along with Brandon and Greg. Jeremy turned on his spotlight and handed the microphone to Maya. She took a deep breath and turned on the microphone switch.

"Edgewood High students! May we please have your attention," she called, forcing a wide smile. "Tonight, we are happy to welcome you to the Edgewood Back-to-School Fashion Slam."

Jeremy pressed the play button and the disco sound pounded through the large speakers on both sides of the runway.

"And now, our head cheerleader, Meg DeLoss." The spotlight found Meg and followed her as she pranced down the runway. Maya read mechanically from her note cards, describing Meg's outfit in a voice that sounded like it was miles away. The next cheerleader made her walk, and Maya read on, fighting back the tidal wave of misery that was crashing down around her on all sides.

"Next we have Brandon Gallagher and Greg Muir," Maya said as the two muscle men strolled down the runway. "Greg and Brandon are wearing the latest fashions from Pramdi of New York."

It was funny how much those two guys had changed in Maya's eyes. At first, they had seemed so awesome—in all their buff, tan, and popular glory. *They're not real,* Maya thought. *What was I thinking?* Greg and Brandon would never be her first choice for friends, she decided.

As they walked off the end of the runway, Jeremy brought the spotlight back to the beginning of the line.

"Maya!" It was a completely panic-stricken Jared, pulling on her sleeve. "Morgan is in the locker room, throwing up."

Throwing up? The magazine article on eating disorders flashed into Maya's brain: throwing up, purging, bulimia.

Bulimia! That tired look on Morgan's face! *What have I done to my baby sister?* Maya thought in horror. *And the way I criti-*

cized her, belittled her for not losing weight for weeks! What have I done to the sweetest kid on the planet?

Maya saw Greg returning to the podium. "Greg!" Maya shouted. "Take the mike."

An astonished Greg looked at the mike in his hand as Maya pushed past him and ran toward the locker room. God had made Morgan a beautiful person, giving her the sweetest temperament and the most radiant smile. And yet Maya had completely ignored Morgan's real beauty.

When Maya burst through the locker room door, Bren, Alex, and Jamie jumped as if a cannon had just gone off. Maya saw Morgan leaning over the sink, one hand gripping the edge.

"Morgan!" Maya shouted, rushing over to her sister.

Morgan looked over her shoulder and smiled weakly. Her face was wet and she was wiping her mouth with a paper towel.

"I'm so sorry!" Maya said, her voice breaking. She grabbed Morgan and threw her arms around her.

"Watch out, Maya," Morgan said, pulling away. "I'm all wet."

Maya pulled her sister even closer. "Who cares about that? Morgan, this is all my fault. My beautiful baby sister is bulimic, and it's all my fault."

Amber started to speak. "Bulimic? You mean where the person throws up on purpose?"

"I never meant for this to happen," Maya replied. "I just got so carried away. But it's like you wrote on the Web site: beauty should come from inside us. This superficial stuff is crazy. Only inner beauty never disappears—"

Morgan looked at Maya with amazed eyes. "Maya, I—"

"Please don't make any more excuses for me," Maya said. "What I did was wrong. And there's no excuse for it. God gave me a beautiful sister. Promise me you'll never try to throw up again."

Morgan chortled. "Are you for real? There is no way I would throw up on purpose. I did try to stop eating so I would be sure and fit into this outfit. And after living on Diet Pepsi for two days, then carrying all of those platforms this morning, I've been pretty dizzy.

"I took one look at the refreshment table and those chocolate eclairs and, well, I probably shouldn't have eaten anything gooey and sweet. But I did. Three of 'em. I barely made it back to the locker room before I threw up."

Morgan stopped and grinned. "But there is no way that I have an eating disorder. As soon as I feel a little better, I'm going to eat something that won't upset my stomach. This starving business is for the birds!"

Maya forced a smile and hugged her sister. Then she looked at her friends.

"I'm so sorry about all of this," Maya said. "I don't know how I let a fashion show become more important than my best friends."

"Speaking of fashion shows," Bren said. "Shouldn't you be getting back out there?"

Maya waved her wrist at the show going on outside. "I've had more than enough fashion for one night. Greg can announce the rest of the show."

"Aren't you forgetting something?" Amber asked. "You still have a few friends who haven't gotten a chance to strut their stuff!"

Maya was dumbfounded. After all the hurt feelings and angry words of the last week, her friends still wanted to be a part of the show?

They all tumbled back into the gym, where Greg seemed elated to hand the microphone back to Maya.

"Our next model is also the president of the junior class. Please welcome Amber Thomas, as she strolls elegantly in a pair of beige chinos and a rust-colored, square necked cotton sweater."

The students applauded as Amber casually walked down the runway.

"Tonight Bren Mickler is wearing an adorable wheat-colored jean skirt that is perfect for a day in the classroom or an autumn afternoon in the stadium watching football. To complete her look, she has chosen a pastel-striped cotton top that is both comfortable and goes great layered, or beneath a sweater. Thank you, Bren."

The audience clapped and Maya went limp with relief. *This is so cool, just like I thought it would be. Only it's nothing like I thought it would be.* And somehow, that was even better.

"Now we turn our attention to Jamie Chandler," Maya continued. "Jamie is wearing what most of us will be wearing to school this fall: jeans. And Jamie's straight-legged jeans come from Levi-Strauss, with a baseball shirt that sets off a casual look both comfortable and easy to care for. I think she looks great. Wouldn't you agree?"

The audience applauded, and Maya saw Jamie smile shyly. For someone as shy as Jamie, Maya decided, that applause could only make her feel more confident. *And hey*, Maya asked herself, *isn't that what friends are for?*

She felt someone tap her shoulder. It was Morgan with Jared!

"Are you feeling good enough to do this?" Maya whispered. Morgan nodded. "And now, for a truly elegant, yet sporty look, Morgan Cross wears black velvet overalls with more fashion jewels than the royal family," Maya said. "Escorting her tonight is the totally cool Jared McElwain, in his hottest, baggiest Union Bay shorts and L2 tee-shirt."

The crowd roared in approval and applause. Jared smiled and held out his arm. Morgan took his arm and walked down the runway as effortlessly as if she did this sort of thing every day of her life.

"And now I would like to conclude tonight's program by inviting everyone who wants to come up to please show us how great you look," Maya said. "Does anybody out there want to make their own fashion statement?"

Several students volunteered, and Maya encouraged them to

stroll down the runway. Then, just at the last moment, Alex stepped out of the crowd and onto the runway. The audience went wild as she two-stepped down the "catwalk" in cowboy boots, leather chaps, and a huge cowboy hat, waving sparklers in each hand. Resounding cheers and applause gave way to Maya, as she thanked the audience for their enthusiasm.

"See you guys in the halls on Monday," she said. "And remember: no matter how great we look on the outside, it's our inner beauty that really counts. Thanks and good night."

Maya clicked off the microphone and breathed in a sigh of relief. After all the blunders she had made, how could this have turned out so well?

Morgan, Bren, Alex, Amber, and Jamie were waiting for her by the main gym door. Maya grinned and took a deep breath.

"I know I've got a lot of explaining to do," Maya said hesitantly. "But can I do it over a pizza at the Gnosh Pit? I'm starving!"

Net Ready, Set, Go!

I hope my words and thoughts please you.
Psalm 19:14

The characters of TodaysGirls.com chat online in the safest—and maybe most fun—of all chat rooms! They've created their own private Web site and room! Many Christian teen sites allow you to create your own private chat rooms, and there are other safe options.

Work with your parents to develop a list of safe, appropriate chat rooms. Earn Internet freedom by showing them you can make the right choices. *Honor your father and your mother (Deuteronomy 5:16).*

Before entering a chat room, you'll select a user name. Although you can use your real name, a nickname is safer. Most people choose one that says something about who they are, like Amber's name, faithful1. Don't be discouraged if the name you select is already taken. You can use a similar one by adding a number at its end.

No one will notice your grammar in a chat room. Don't worry if you spell something wrong or forget to capitalize. Some people even misspell words on purpose. You might see a sentence like How R U?

But sometimes it's important to be accurate. Web site and e-mail addresses must be exact. Pay close attention to whether letters are upper- or lowercase. Remember that Web site addresses don't use some punctuation marks, such as hyphens and apostrophes. (That's why the "Today's" in TodaysGirls.com has no apostrophe!) And instead of spaces between words, underlines are used to_make_a_space. And sometimes words just run together like onebigword.

R U 4 Real?

When you're in a chat room, remember real people are typing the words that appear on your screen. Treat them with the same respect you expect from them. Don't say anything you wouldn't want repeated in Sunday school. *Do for other people what you want them to do for you (Luke 6:31).*

Sometimes people say mean, hurtful things—things that make us angry. This can happen in chat rooms, too. In some chat rooms, you can highlight a rude person's name and click a button that says, "ignore," which will make his or her comments disappear from your screen. You always have the option to switch rooms or sign off. If a particular person becomes a continual problem, or if someone says something especially vicious, you should report this problem user to the chat service. *Ask God to bless those who say bad things to you. Pray for those who are cruel (Luke 6:28–29).*

Remember that Internet information is not always factual. Whether you're chatting or surfing Web sites, be skeptical about information and people. Not everything on the Internet is true. You don't have to be afraid of the Internet, but you should always be cautious. Practice caution with others even in Christian chat rooms.

It's okay to chat about your likes and dislikes, but *never* give out personal information. Do not tell anyone your name, phone number, address, or even the name of your school, team, church, or neighborhood. Be cautious. . . . *You will be like sheep among wolves. So be as smart as snakes. But also be like doves and do nothing wrong. Be careful of people (Matthew 10:16–17).*

STRANGER ONLINE

AMBER
THOMAS

16/junior
e-name: faithful1
best friend: Maya
site area: Thought for the Day

Confident. Caring. Swimmer. Single-handedly built
TodaysGirls.com Web site. Loves her folks.
Big brother Ryan drives her nuts! Great friend.
Got a problem? Go to Amber.

JAMIE CHANDLER

PORTRAIT OF LIES

15/sophomore
e-name: rembrandt
best friend: Bren
site area: Artist's Corner

Quiet. Talented artist. Works at the Gnosh Pit
after school. Dad left when she was little.
Helps her mom with younger sisters Jordan and
Jessica. Babysits for Coach Short's kids.

ALEX DIAZ

TANGLED WEB

14/freshman
e-name: TX2step
best friend: Morgan
site area: to be determined . . .

Spicy. Hot-tempered Texan. Lives with grandparents because
of parents' problems. Won state in freestyle swimming at her
old school. Snoops. Into everything. Breaks the rules.

R U 4 REAL?

16/junior
e-name: nycbutterfly
best friend: Amber
site area: What's Hot—What's Not

Fashion freak. Health nut. Grew up in New York City.
Small town drives her crazy. Loves to dance.
Dad owns the Gnosh Pit. Little sis Morgan is also
a TodaysGirl.

MAYA CROSS

BREN MICKLER

LUV@FIRST SITE

15/sophomore
e-name: chicChick
best friend: Jamie
site area: Smashin' Fashion

Funny. Popular. Outgoing. Spaz. Cheerleader. Always late.
Only child. Wealthy family. Bren is chatting—
about anything, online and off, except when
she's eating junk food.

CHAT FREAK

14/freshman
e-name: jellybean
best friend: Alex
site area: Feeling All Write (under construction)

The Web-ster. Spends too much time online. Overalls.
M&Ms. Swim team. Tries to save the world. Close to her
family—when her big sister isn't bossing her around.

MORGAN
CROSS

Cyber Glossary

Bounced mail An e-mail that has been returned to its sender.

Chat A live conversation—typed or spoken through microphones—among individuals in a chat room.

Chat room A "place" on the Internet where individuals meet to "talk" with one another.

Crack To break a security code.

Download To receive information from a more powerful computer.

E-mail Electronic mail which is sent through the Internet.

E-mail address An Internet address where e-mail is received.

File Any document or image stored on a computer.

Floppy Disk A small, thin plastic object which stores information to be accessed by a computer.

Hacker Someone who tries to gain unauthorized access to another computer or network of computers.

Header Text at the beginning of an e-mail which identifies the sender, subject matter, and the time at which it was sent.

Homepage A Web site's first page.

Internet A worldwide electronic network that connects computers to each other.

Link Highlighted text or a graphic element which may be clicked with the mouse in order to "surf" to another Web site or page.

Log on/Log in To connect to a computer network.

Modem A device which enables computers to exchange information.

The Net The Internet.

Newbie A person who is learning or participating in something new.

Online To have Internet access. Can also mean to use the Internet.

Surf To move from page to page through links on the Web.

The Web The World Wide Web or WWW.

Upload To send information to a more powerful computer.